Winner Books are produced
designed to entertain and
Christian principles. Each b
specialists in Christian educat
These books uphold the tea
Bible.

Other Winner Books you will enjoy:

MARGARET EPP was born into a large family in Waldheim, Saskatchewan. She spent six years of her early childhood in China, where her parents served as missionaries with the China Mennonite Mission Society. Illness forced them to return to Canada, where they settled on a farm.

Miss Epp is a graduate of Bethany Bible Institute in Hepburn, Saskatchewan and attended Prairie Bible Institute in Three Hills, Alberta. For 30 years she has specialized in writing books for children and young people.

SARAH AND THE LOST FRIENDSHIP

Margaret Epp

A WINNER BOOK

VICTOR
BOOKS a division of SP Publications, Inc.
WHEATON. ILLINOIS 60187

Offices also in
Whitby, Ontario, Canada
Amersham-on-the-Hill, Bucks, England

Third printing, 1983

All Scripture quotations are from the King James Version.

Library of Congress Catalog Card No. 78-65203
ISBN: 0-88207-483-0

VICTOR BOOKS
A division of SP Publications, Inc.
P.O. Box 1825 • Wheaton, Ill. 60187

Contents

CHAPTER 1
Back to School Day

SOMETIMES YOU WISH very much for something to happen—and then it does happen. And then you wish with all your heart that it hadn't. That's what Sarah Naomi Scott discovered.

It was January 4, 1926—the first day of school in a brand new year.

The day began for Sarah with this golden ball staring and staring at her. Sarah frowned, squinching up her eyes. But it still kept staring. Then it turned into a lamp, her very own flowery lamp, sitting on her own table. Oh! Mother must have been up here to light the lamp and to awaken her. But she couldn't remember a thing about it!

That minute, Mother's call came drifting up the stairs with the smell of cooking oatmeal. "Sarah? Sarah Scott! Are you up? Remember, school starts today."

Ooh! Aah! Sarah yawned. She began stretching her arms but jerked them back under the comforter in a hurry. Brr! The room was icy. And her clothes were out of reach. So how was she ever going to get dressed?

School! January 4. No more holidays with neighbors dropping in at any old time—for dinner or supper—and staying hours and hours. Playing games like charades maybe, or Button, Button, Who's got the button? Or just sitting there, telling stories, or singing around the organ.

Except for one thing, these Christmas holidays had been the best of all. That one thing was that Sarah's sister Kathleen, married now and living way off in California, had had to go and miss all the fun. Imagine! No snow. No ice. She and Herbie could buy apples and make popcorn maybe. But it wasn't the same—not the same at all as skating on the pond all afternoon or coasting down the hill, with a million billion stars sparkling on the pastures and the giant strawstack and on the trees and boulders along the creek.

And always and always this Christmas there'd been Keith, her handsome big brother! He left home when she was only four—and now he'd been back less than two weeks. But sometimes she had this feeling that she and he had been friends all their lives. He was a lot of fun—*most* of the time. Each day his cough was getting less and I—

"Sarah Naomi Scott! What's the matter with you today? Must I come up and dress you?" called Mother.

Wow-whee! She meant business this time!

Sarah jumped from bed, made a dive for her heap of clothes, scooped up her moccasins and scampered across the creaking wood floor. It was so cold it seared the soles of her bare feet.

She blew a big puff across the lamp chimney. Out. Then she skimmed through the door and down the stairs as warm air rushed up to meet her. Mother, standing over the cookstove, shook her head at her. Stuart sat alone at the table, eating breakfast. He'd be leaving for Blakely High School any minute now. Just as Sarah scooted into the parlor, Father and Robbie came into the kitchen bringing rushing clouds of cold air with them, and four foaming pails of milk.

"Why, you slowpoke!" called Robbie. "Better get a wiggle on."

She giggled as she slammed the parlor door. Ooh! Lovely in here, warm and lovely. She didn't need a lamp because the heater had mica doors, and the firelight flickered through them and over the walls and furniture.

But she couldn't dawdle. Not on a school day. One dreadful day last fall she and Robbie were late to school —a whole half hour! She wouldn't ever, ever want that to happen again. So she burrowed and wiggled her way into her clothes. The scratchy serge dress—last winter's Sunday best—came over the soft flannel things. Then the heavy woolen stockings, and the elastic garters— Ugh! Tight! Last of all the moccasins. She laced them with fingers that shook a bit because she could hear the purr of the cream separator slowing down. When Father was finished with that job she had better be at her place, all properly dressed. That's the way things were at the Scott house. But poking rawhide thongs through little holes wasn't easy.

There. Done!

"Almost didn't make it," said Robbie severely when she slid into her chair.

"That will do, Robbie," said Mother quietly. Then she half whispered. "Your hair, Sarah! Matted as a mouse's nest!"

But then everyone settled down to listen to Father reading the morning chapter. Even Stuart, who was all ready to leave for Blakely. He sank into the chair nearest the outer door, over where the coats and jackets hung on hooks.

A lamp sat in the middle of the table. Heat from it warmed Sarah's forehead and cheeks. It lit up Father's face—and Mother's—and Keith's hand, where he sat shading his face.

Father read a psalm. (*Good*, thought Sarah. Usually they weren't as long as other chapters of the Bible.) This one began, "I will bless the Lord at all times: His praise shall continually be in my mouth" (Ps. 34). And on to, "This poor man cried, and the Lord heard him, and saved him out of all his troubles."

A diamond flashed. Then it rolled slowly down Keith's cheek and onto his sweater, where it blinked at Sarah. She had this funny feeling—warm and sad and glad all mixed together. Keith's hand never moved. Sarah didn't know if anyone else had noticed.

Father was reading now: "O taste and see that the Lord is good: blessed is the man that trusteth in Him."

Along with the others, Sarah ducked her head when Father prayed. He was praying for all of them—for Kathleen and Herbie way off in California, where Herbie was studying to become a preacher. And for all of them here. His voice got husky when he thanked God again for bringing Keith home to them—most of all for making him a child of God!

The diamond was gone when they raised their heads again.

Over at the washbasin Sarah gave her face and hands a quick scrub, and ran the comb over her hair a few times. Mother would have to rake out the tangles later. Keith helped Sarah to oatmeal porridge, teasing her as he did so. And Mother brought a plateful of toast, and mugfuls of hot milk for Sarah and Robbie.

"Eat and be off with you," she said. "Yes, the lunch pails are packed. A pity if you should begin the new school year by being late."

After breakfast and after Mother had done her hair. Sarah crowded into her school overcoat. For a long moment then she stood looking down at herself in despair. Mother had let it out and let it down two months ago, but you wouldn't know it.

Robbie grinned at her on his way to the door. "Ichabod Crane," he teased.

Well, Sarah wasn't in grade eight like Robbie, but she knew all about Ichabod Crane—the schoolmaster that Washington Irving wrote about, the one whose hands dangled a mile out of his sleeves.

"You just be quiet, Robbie Scott!" wailed Sarah. "I can't *help* it that my coat is too small."

She had *begged* to be allowed to wear the new one—a Christmas present from Keith. Heather mixture tweed! With fur collar and cuffs. Really elegant, even if the fur was only white rabbit. You could pretend it was ermine just like all the knights and their ladies wore in the olden days.

Grown-ups are funny. Mother had said no, and again *no!* Very firmly. Now she was looking at Sarah in a strange way.

Beyond her at the table Father had made a teepee of his hands, hiding his mouth. Above it his eyes twinkled, and his shoulders shook ever so slightly. But Keith was plainly grinning at Sarah.

"Wear your new coat," said Mother. "I'll have to see what I can do about this one. And hurry, child. Is that Robbie at the gate? Don't keep Wally waiting out in the cold."

Sarah had a last-minute scramble to find her new pencil box, and the exercise books and slate. Clutching them in her mittened hands, she ran out to where Wally, the school horse, was pawing the snow impatiently. The mittens were red and didn't match the coat. Neither did the moccasins and her patched rubbers. But that didn't matter—much.

Sarah hopped into the sleigh, tucked the buffalo robe around her knees, and pulled the fur collar close to her cheeks. Soft. Cozy as anything. In a minute her eyelashes were starched stiff with frost; and when they swung to face the wind, the cold clamped down on her forehead. But the rest of her was warm as could be.

They didn't talk much, she and Robbie. He'd whistled at the sight of her coat, but now his mackinaw collar was up, his chin drawn in, and his face turning purplish red in the wind.

The trail was wide and shiny smooth from all the sleigh tracks made during the holidays. Wally had a lumbering trot, but he could cover ground. Sitting so low down made it seem really fast. And today Wally's hooves picked up balls of snow and flung them right and left. At every corner he broke into a stiff little gallop, and each time the sleigh slithered in a wide arc that sent prickles and tickles chasing one another through Sarah's middle. Maybe Wally was tired of the do-nothing holidays. Maybe he was glad to be going back to school, even if it meant standing in his dark stall all day.

In a way Sarah was glad too. In a few minutes she'd see Susan Gerrick, her friend—and Kathleen's sister-in-law. And today she'd meet a teacher with a new name. Not a new teacher, but a new name. Miss Haliday was Mrs. Grant Millar now. She and Grace Millar's bachelor brother had been married in Ontario during the holidays. So that was one new thing. And then there was Sarah's coat. If the school wasn't sufficiently warmed up on this

first school day morning, maybe, just maybe, she'd be allowed to wear it all through the first period!

Wally broke into a gallop again because they were nearing the school corner. Just too late Robbie noticed the big snowdrift that had piled up inside the gate. It happened so fast. One instant Sarah sat snugly, collecting the slate and things in her mittens, ready to jump out of the cutter. The next she sprawled face down in the drift, gasping and coughing. She was blinded by snow. She fought, making swimming motions, because her hands and knees kept breaking through the crust.

She heard a splintering sound and a confusion of shouts. Something slammed against her, knocking her flat again, and scraping over her. When she came up finally, spitting and coughing, she saw Wally climbing over hillocks of snow. Snow lay in patches on his flank, and the sleigh dragged awkwardly behind him because the shafts were broken.

But that wasn't the worst of it.

Her slate was smashed to smithereens. Her exercise books were torn and bedraggled. Her lovely new pencil box had sprung open and had sprayed her crayons and pencils, her penholders and erasers, into the jumble of snow.

But that wasn't the worst either.

On the right sleeve of her new coat, up where *everybody* would see it, was a big three-cornered tear.

It can't be true—and it mustn't be true, thought Sarah numbly.

She had this dead and gone feeling as she knelt in the snow, picking up broken halves of crayons. (Her new crayons—a Christmas present from Robbie.) Somehow she couldn't see clearly.

If only her coat were hanging in the upstairs closet at home. Safe. New. Lovely. It would never, never look the same again—

"Sarah? Sarah, dear, are you hurt?" came an anxious voice. Teacher's voice, warm and sympathetic. "Oh, my dear! Too bad about the coat—but we'll see what we can do about that sleeve later. Come. You're sure you're not hurt?"

Now that she began walking she knew she was, a bit. One knee was skinned. It was beginning to burn fiercely, and Sarah was almost glad for an excuse to shed a few tears as she limped up the porch steps.

Miss Haliday—no, *Mrs. Millar*—was nice as could be to her. In the girls' coatroom she laid a pad of cooling ointment over the knee so the stocking couldn't rub the sore place.

But Susan Gerrick—Sarah's *friend*—said, "Well, why *did* you wear your good coat? Mother never lets me. She says a good manager doesn't allow it."

"M-my m-mother's a g-good m-manager," said Sarah, her dark eyes flashing through tears. "As g-good as yours, Susan Gerrick! S-so th-there!"

"Hush, dear," said Teacher soothingly. "Susan, ring the bell for me, will you?" And then, when she and Sarah were alone in the coatroom, she smiled at Sarah and whispered.

"We'll have that coat looking as good as new again. Really. I mean it. Fortunately it's a tweed—and fortunately too my mother is a professional mender of clothes—"

"But—but she's way off in Ontario!"

Mrs. Millar laughed. "She took considerable pains to teach me her craft. Trust me. Wait and see."

The bell rang. Girls came trooping up the basement stairs, and boys came galloping in from outdoors. They shrugged off their coats and jackets and kicked off their rubbers and overshoes. They clunked their dinner pails onto the shelf and slammed their books onto their desks. Then the noises hushed as Braeburn pupils lined up in the aisles, the grade-eight pupils in the rear and the other grades in the front. Four irregular stepladders stood facing Teacher.

"Good morning, boys and girls," she said.

"Good morning, Mrs. Millar!" came the answering chorus.

Some looked sheepish. Some grinned. Some forgot, and said "Miss Haliday—" and blushed and giggled with embarrassment. But Sarah Scott stood on her left foot, with her right knee slightly bent. Her sad and worried thoughts were on the coat.

Would Teacher really be able to mend it? *Good as new* she'd said. But Sarah was afraid to hope. It was hard to keep her mind on her studies during the first period, even if reading was her very most favorite subject.

When recess came the coat had disappeared from the coatroom. And because Sarah couldn't play outdoors with the rest today, Teacher asked her to dust the library shelves and books. This was special. Usually only grade-eight girls got to do this for Teacher.

The room was quiet. Sarah could hear a lot of shouting and squealing from the yard where Braeburn was playing Prisoner's Base. And she could hear Teacher speaking softly into the telephone.

"*Please,* darling," Sarah heard her coaxing. Imagine saying "darling" to Grant Millar! "I *know* you can do it."

Grace Millar always said her brother was awfully nice and clever, and that he read heaps of books and knew— oh, ever so many fascinating things about nature. But he was sort of shy and had a big nose with bushy eyebrows meeting on the bridge. People had always treated him as a sort of joke—until Miss Haliday up and married him!

"I *knew* I could count on you," Sarah heard her say softly.

When the second period began, Braeburn had a surprise. Well, it was more like a shock, really. Grant Millar had come to school! Teacher, her cheeks pink, introduced "my husband" to the pupils and then she walked from the room. Sarah, who had half guessed what was going to happen, heard the jingle of trace chains as Teacher drove away, leaving her pupils to this big shy farmer.

But he did all right. If the big boys expected to make a fool of him, well, they soon forgot. Grant Millar could do about 50 birdcalls! And he could tell stories of coyotes and beaver, of owls and hawks—real stories, clever stories —and every single one had happened on his own farm!

The boys and girls sat there, hardly stirring, until suddenly someone noticed that it was two minutes past twelve. Dinnertime. Hoo! A few of them stretched their arms and shuffled their feet.

Grant Millar rose from where he'd been perching on the desk corner, and he looked along the road to his farm. That minute Sarah heard trace chains jingling.

Oh, dear Lord, let the coat be all right again! she prayed, her heart jerking in a funny way.

Teacher stood in the doorway. "Thanks, darling," she said breathlessly. In front of everybody! Then, "Class dismissed."

Desks slammed and pupils stampeded to the hall to pick out their dinner pails. Sarah stood rooted. Teacher laid the coat in her arms, but Sarah hardly needed to glance at the sleeve. Teacher's eyes were sparkling. That was almost enough proof.

The sleeve was whole again. If you knew about the tear, and if you looked really close, you could faintly see where it had been. But that was all.

Sarah didn't know if she was laughing or crying. She hugged the coat, and she wished she dared to hug Teacher. "You're wonderful! You're the best there is!" she exclaimed.

"No arguments from me on that, Sarah Scott," said the big farmer, smiling.

CHAPTER 2
Two Letters for Sarah

THE WIND WAS still blowing from the west when school was over that day. All the way home Wally wouldn't need to face into it; that was one good thing. The splintered shafts had been bound up. Grant Millar did that so they would last until Father could really fix them. And Sarah's coat was good as new.

So why wasn't she feeling happier?

It wasn't because of the darkness, nor the snow that hissed across their tracks.

Wally trotted along in the left-hand trail. You couldn't see much beyond his rump on that side. But everywhere around lay murky white fields, and blurry black patches when you passed the leafless bushes, and faint snaky trails here and there leading to farmyards. You could make out dark huddles of buildings beyond, and perhaps a pinpoint of light in the farmhouse. And of course you could hear dogs barking, and perhaps a calf bawling.

This was ordinary. This was the way it was every day. So why did all of it make Sarah feel sad today?

Robbie had finished munching a frozen sandwich, left over from noon.

"Want mine?" offered Sarah, listlessly.

"Sure, if you don't want it. Hey, something wrong?"

How could she tell him? It was such a little thing—a

stupid thing—a girl thing. It wasn't really a quarrel at all.

During noon recess she had been alone in the coatroom, feeling the mended sleeve, glad about it, when she heard the big girls talking to Susan. They were teasing her again. She was easy to tease. She always took things so seriously.

Suddenly Violetta Siddons called out, "Hey, Sarah Scott, did you hear that?"

The Siddons didn't own much—not even a farm. They were only renters. They probably were the poorest family in Braeburn. But Mrs. Siddons was awfully good at choosing fancy names when her babies were born. Sarah thought Violetta was a very elegant name. But today, when she came hopping into the schoolroom in answer to Violetta's call, she wasn't thinking of how common her own name sounded. Susan Gerrick was fighting to hold Violetta's mouth shut. That was the first thing she noticed. The bigger girl wrenched her chin free, and she laughed and called out, "Did you hear, Sarah? Susan says Kathleen is more her sister than yours."

"I did not."

"You did so!"

"I did not! I said *I* was as much her sister as Sarah. *In a way.* That's what I said."

"It's the same thing," said Violetta, laughing harder than ever.

Sarah wasn't laughing. "In what way?" she demanded.

"Well, she's a Gerrick. Same as me. And you're a Scott. She's Mrs. Herbert Gerrick, so there!"

Sarah noticed the big girls winking at one another Some sided with Sarah and some with Susan. They didn't really care; it was just a way to have fun. So Sarah surprised them. She hopped away. No big girls were going to make her fight with anybody.

All the same, she thought as she slid into her desk. *All the same, Susan had better watch what she says!*

Teacher had given Sarah four new exercise books to take the place of the torn, soiled ones. Sarah ran her hands over the smooth clean pages, and she sighed a bit. She *liked* neat things. So why couldn't she ever keep her scribblers as neat as Susan kept hers?

That Susan! Right now she was reading a letter aloud— a letter from Kathleen. Sarah had read it before. It was just a nice sister-in-law sort of letter. Sarah hadn't minded before, not the least bit. Now, suddenly, she had this crawling feeling under her skin.

Susan's voice was raised and went sort of straight along, the way it always did in reading class. She never had much expression.

"My dear little sister," she read. "How are you today? Herbie and I were glad to get your Christmas letter. Herbie wants to know if the hens are laying well this winter. And how many cows have freshened, and how many pailfuls of milk you average each day. Are prices for eggs and cream steady this winter? We are interested in every detail, remember that. . . ."

"*Hoo!*" thought Sarah impatiently.

Just then Teacher came into the room to shoo the girls out, all except Sarah, who could remain indoors because of her sore knee. She hobbled to the library and spent the rest of the noon hour and all of the afternoon recess happily with Jo March and her sisters. This was the second time she was reading *Little Women*.

She never could decide which of the four she liked best. Not Meg. She was too grownup and proper. And not Amy. She was sort of stuck-up. But Beth was the one you loved and *loved,* and Jo was the one who could make you laugh.

In fact, Sarah had felt quite cheerful as long as school lasted. Why did she feel so sort of grumpy now? She wished Wally would speed up, but he just kept up his sleepy trot.

Suddenly, sharp on the air, came a familiar bark. Spencer! They were almost home.

The yard was full of gray darkness and dim moving shapes and quiet familiar sounds. The squeak of the windmill and the gush of water into the trough. The creak of cows' hocks and the crunch of snow under their hooves. The jingle-jangle of trace chains and the snorting of horses. Father had just got back from Blakely. Sarah could see him leading Prince and Captain toward the barn. She hopped from the sleigh—quite forgetting to hobble!—and went skimming toward the house. Warm yellow light from the kitchen window seemed to hold welcoming arms out to her.

In the kitchen Keith had just lighted the lantern. He was dressed in his choring clothes. He helped her and Robbie with the milking each evening now. But he waited to hear her story of today's happenings.

When Mother heard about the accident and the torn sleeve, she was as horrified as Sarah had known she'd be. And then, when she saw the place, she couldn't believe it had been so bad—not until she turned the sleeve inside out and examined the mending. She shook her head too over Sarah's skinned knee, and guessed she'd better stay indoors tonight.

But this didn't suit Sarah at all. She loved the cozy times with Keith.

"Father brought you two letters from town," said Mother almost coaxingly.

Two? One from Linda Bolton—one from Kathleen!

Sarah's fingers shook as she ripped open the second envelope. "My dear little sister," the letter began.

Just the same, thought Sarah numbly. *It begins just the same way as Susan's. Then maybe Kathleen loves her just the same too. Or better.*

Ah, no. But anyway, she might love Susan's *letters* better. Because, Sarah would never even *think* of writing about how much milk they got, and about the price of cream and eggs. That wasn't the sort of thing she ever felt like writing to Kathleen!

Sarah tucked the letter away unread, and opened the other. Her eyes skipped down the page. Linda was learning to walk. Really! Linda, her very best friend who lived in Ontario now—who had had infantile paralysis some years ago, and who'd had these rag-doll legs ever since. Well, not anymore!

Sarah forgot about her own sore knee. Holding the letter up, she whirled around and around. "Linda can walk —she can walk—she can walk!" she chanted.

Mother said, "You're sure?"

And Father, who had just come in, added, "Praise the Lord!"

"She walked two steps," said Sarah proudly.

Linda had added that she fell flat on her face when she tried to take a third step, but she made it sound like a joke. And pretty soon she'd be *really* walking. Sarah just *knew* it.

She was so happy over Linda, she chattered about her all the way to the barn with Keith. The lantern swung between them. She told him about the girl who came to stay with Aunt Jane Bolton on the neighboring farm. Maybe Keith had heard it all before, but sometimes you can't help repeating.

The lantern lit up the gray, hard-packed snowpath and Sarah's flared skirt, made from Father's old overalls. Her shiny rubber overshoes twinkled in the light as she skipped along. Her knee hurt, but not much.

The barn was dim and warm and moist, the way it usually was at milking time. Speckles, the hen, sat on Brindle's back as usual too. The cow was her foot warmer!

They were friends. Twice the Scotts had tried penning Speckles up with the other hens in the chicken house. But she had crouched near the door all day, making sad, mourning sounds, and refusing to lay any eggs. Brindle was restless too, without her. So Father had decided the friends belonged together.

Each night Speckles perched on Brindle's back. Each day she laid an egg in Brindle's crib. Tonight, as usual, Sarah hurried to scoop up the egg before Robbie filled the crib with feed for the cows.

There is something cozy about a warm barn on a winter night. You hear the horses stamping as they pull their oat sheaves apart, and the crunch of their strong teeth as they eat the stalks. And there's the low crooning of the newest baby calf in its pen, and the half-groaning sound of cows breathing, and the swish-swish of milk streams striking the foam. Sarah was getting to be pretty good at milking. Well, Brindle was a good cow to milk; she let her milk down easily.

Father whistled softly as he carried chopped feed to the horses. Stuart had just returned from Blakely High School. He was unharnessing Hyacinth.

"Well, Princess," said Keith. (Except for Father, he was the only one who called her that!) "What are you so busy about?"

"Me? Busy? Why—I'm—I'm *milking*."

He laughed. "I meant, what were you thinking about? You've been so quiet." Then he sighed. "Know something, sis? I wish I were about your age again."

"Ten years old? Why, Keith?"

When he answered, which was after a moment, the laughter had gone from his voice. "Because this time around I wouldn't waste my years. Believe me, *this time around*, I'd finish high school."

"Only—" said Sarah, half puzzled and half fascinated at the idea, "there can't be more than one time around, can there?"

"You're so right! So where does that leave me? A washout. A failure!"

Oh, no! Sarah thought.

"Halfway through high school—and I had to throw it all aside. Now it's too late," said Keith.

That was an awfully sad thought—*too late*. But, one exciting idea teased Sarah. It wasn't too late! Not really. It needn't be. He was still alive, and he could read! You could learn *anything* out of books!

"Well—" Keith rose. "That's that. I'm through here. How about you?"

"Finished." Because of this buzzing idea and all, Sarah pushed the stool so hard that it tumbled into the gutter. She and the milk pail almost went tumbling after it. Keith caught and steadied her.

"Oops there. All right now?"

She didn't even bother to say thank you. "Keith, you could finish now, couldn't you?" she said breathlessly. "High school, I mean. All the things you've got to know —they're in books, aren't they? So why don't you—"

Keith laughed shortly. "At my age? Where would I begin?"

"Why—" She looked up at him helplessly. "Why, right here. Now."

He stood there looking at her, with the lantern shining in his eyes and a pail of foaming milk, hanging from each hand. Just then Sarah noticed that Father had come up behind her. He had begun rubbing her tam because he couldn't rub her hair! He did that when he was pleased with her.

But he spoke to Keith. "That might be the answer, Keith. I shouldn't wonder. Stuart still has all the books, and he'd be glad to explain any difficult part. Or the principal would—or your mother could help. If one were not too proud—"

"Too proud to *learn?*" broke in Sarah, astonished.

Keith smiled down on her. "You love learning?"

"I want to—to gobble it up," she said. "I want never to stop—not as long as I live!"

Father laughed. "Well said," he commented as he took the lantern from its hook and gave the sliding door a shove with his elbow. The squeaking casters—they were part of the choring sounds too.

Then they went indoors for supper.

The kitchen was sort of crowded tonight because Mother had been sewing today. That is, she had dug up one of Grandfather Murray's overcoats, and had opened all the seams of Sarah's old coat to use it as a pattern, sort of. But things weren't working out too happily.

There was a lot of material in Grandfather's coat, but still it wouldn't do. It didn't look right for a little girl, for one thing. The pockets and buttonholes all came at the wrong places, Mother said. Suddenly she groaned, bundled all the stuff together, pushed it into a cardboard box, and dusted her hands. "I give up," she said.

Everybody breathed a bit more freely, it seemed to Sarah. When Mother had a sewing puzzle on her hands, nothing seemed to go exactly right in the home. And it might take days and days to sew the coat!

"Does this mean," said Sarah hopefully, "that I get to wear the new coat every day?" (The old one was all taken apart!)

"I suppose so," said Mother. "But don't you go and tear it again tomorrow."

"But that wasn't her fault," said Robbie generously. "If anyone's got to be scolded, I guess it's me. I didn't see the drift in time, so over we went."

Nobody got scolded. Father changed the subject by asking what Kathleen had written, so Sarah couldn't escape reading the letter any longer. And it wasn't so bad! There wasn't a word about cream and egg prices in the entire letter. There *was* something about cows though. This was the way it ran:

"And do you remember our walk together, rounding up the cows, on the morning of my wedding? I think of it often. We spoke about following the Lord Jesus wherever He might lead us. Remember?

"Well, He has led Herbie and me here to school, and we are very happy. Of course, we are sorry to miss getting to know Keith all over again. Give our big brother a hug for me, will you?"

There were three *pages* of it. All full of "do you remember when" bits. A *lovely* letter. All during suppertime— they had beef stew and hashed-brown potatoes and stewed canned tomatoes—the Scotts talked about the letter, and about this new idea that Keith should go back to high school. Actually he'd not be going to school but studying at home. Stuart got really excited. He would help; and so would the principal, he was sure. And others, maybe— Look at the way Louise Thatcher helped him during seeding time last spring!

It seemed to Sarah that everybody looked particularly cheerful tonight. Perhaps all of them had been a bit worried about Keith, worried because he didn't have anything really worthwhile to keep him busy. Except read the Bible, and he did a lot of that. But he wasn't strong enough yet to go chopping wood with Father. Life was so different for him now.

Once Sarah had overheard Father tell Mother of the day when Keith became a Christian. He got right up out of bed, weak as he was, and stepped over to the stove and chucked his pack of cigarettes into the fire. And he hadn't smoked again, not one single time. But twice this week when Sarah awoke at night she had heard him padding downstairs to the water pail for a long, cold drink.

Father and Mother got up too, and she'd heard a murmur of voices till she dropped off to sleep again. When she asked Father about it, he sighed and said that bad habits weren't easy to break, and they'd all have to keep praying for Keith so he'd remain victorious. He was putting up a good fight.

This evening, when Sarah crawled into her rustling strawtick bed, she could hear the rest of the family talking in the kitchen. Her own happy thoughts skipped over the events of the day. A long, long day—getting up *almost* too late (being lazy in the morning was one of her bad habits, she supposed)—and changing into the new coat at the last minute—and that awful, terrible minute when she saw the torn sleeve—and kind Teacher mending it so nicely—and Grant Millar giving that interesting nature talk—and Susan's letter—

Suddenly the happy thoughts came to a full stop.

That Susan Gerrick! Thinking Kathleen was more her sister just because they had the same family name now!

Sarah sighed. Susan's letter from Kathleen wasn't *nearly* as nice as hers.

Thinking fondly of her "do you remember when" letter, Sarah fell asleep.

CHAPTER 3
A Ride
and a Rescue

FATHER SAID that Mother had grown 10 years younger lately. *Since Keith came home.* Maybe she had. Sometimes Sarah had this feeling that Mother had turned into Kathleen, or something.

Like the evening when it was full moon.

There's something about full moon in winter. It was pretty cold out, of course. Almost 20° below zero. But the whole outdoors was practically as bright as day. Coyotes howled on the hill behind the creek, and all the dogs for miles around got excited. It was that kind of evening—shining and singing and clear.

Someone said, "Wouldn't it be a nice evening to go coasting!" And someone else said, "Yes, let's!" And before you knew it, all the Scotts were bundling up. Even Stuart!

There was only one toboggan. But Father got the old stoneboat out of the shed—the one they used in summer to haul barrels of water from the creek to water the garden. It had sturdy wooden runners edged with ribbons of steel for smoothness. And Robbie ran to the granary for the shovel. He could sit cross-legged on that, and go jiggling down, grasping the handle to steer it.

Spencer joined the fun, of course. He always plunged alongside, uphill and down again. That was his idea of a good time. But Sarah didn't know that Ginger had decided to go coasting too, until she saw this brownish shadow trotting beside her on the way from the house.

Ginger was a barn cat but was still a special friend. The snow was too cold for his paws so Sarah picked him up, and he burrowed under her jacket. The next thing Sarah knew, he had poked his wedge-shaped face up over the second button of her jacket.

Laughing, Sarah scooted back to the house. She grabbed an old scarf off a hook on the kitchen wall and tied it around her like a belt, over the jacket but under the bulge that was Ginger. He couldn't slide down now.

He put his paws around her neck and licked her chin, purring like a tiny Fordson tractor. So that's the way Sarah and Ginger went coasting.

Everybody laughed to see the wedge-shaped face under Sarah's chin. Everybody took spills in the snow. There were the long tickling *swooshes* from the top of the hill to the ice-covered creek. Under the moon the snow was the whitest Sarah had ever seen. Each shrub and tree cast a blue shadow. It was like magic.

Afterward they all went uphill, still laughing and talking, but tired now. At the barn Sarah had to coax Ginger before he would leave his comfortable perch inside her jacket. Then she ran to catch up with the rest of the family.

A large kettleful of cocoa waited in the kitchen. Robbie discovered that the bed of coals in the range was just right for popping corn, so he popped a big dishpanful while Sarah melted some butter. And Father said why didn't Stuart go for some Macintosh apples. So they sat sipping and munching and talking.

But nobody lit the lamps; the moonlight came in through the windows, clean and strong. Bright enough to read by. When it was time for family devotions, Father tried it, and it worked.

The next day was Saturday.

Father and Stuart and Robbie drove away right after breakfast to the river hills to chop wood. They had taken the boxes off the bobsleighs so there was nothing left but the double runners and the crossbars and the four corner posts. They took the long-handled frying pan in a gunnysack, and the open kettle, all black with soot. And they took a boxful of stuff—raw sausage, buns, and apples—for their dinner at noon. They planned to be back by suppertime.

Father drove Prince and Captain, and Stuart drove Beauty and Daisy. Robbie just sat on the crosspiece at the rear of Stuart's sleigh, swinging his legs and teasing Spencer. The dog was going with them, of course. Whenever Robbie's feet got cold he could jump off and run alongside his pal for a bit.

Today Sarah wished she were a boy. It wasn't fair! Robbie could go off into the woods and be gone all day. He just *loved* to go. She had to collect eight lamps and fill them, trim the wicks, and wash and polish the globes. After that she was expected to dry the breakfast things. And after that, she had to polish all the family shoes. It just simply wasn't *fair!*

Sarah grumbled as she worked, and finally Mother rebuked her sort of sharply. Keith sat at the table, trying to study. The stove in his room was balky today for no good reason; it kept smoking. So he had his books spread between the lamps and globes and breakfast crumbs. It was a real mix-up.

Keith was having trouble too. He wasn't used to studying math. His geometry problem wouldn't come out right

—and *wouldn't* come right! Mother tried to explain, but she wasn't awfully good at explaining mathematics. Sarah could have told him that, even if she knew nothing about geometry. Mother was more of a grammar and literature sort of person.

Keith kept running his fingers through his hair so that it looked wilder and wilder. Suddenly he pushed back his chair and stood up. He raised his books high and slammed them down on the table. A lamp globe skipped off the table and smashed in a hundred pieces on the floor.

"As far as I'm concerned," he said through his teeth, "these books and all who wrote them can go straight to—" He stopped short.

A prickly sort of silence quivered through the room. Keith— why, he almost— he was going to—*swear*.

But what came next was almost worse. He hung his head, looking terrible. Sarah heard him groan, "Oh, Mother, it's no *use!* I'll never amount to anything."

Sarah was down on her knees picking up bits of glass, and she was trembling. But Mother was splendid. Her face was white, but she smiled. Sort of like the moonlight looked last night.

"Yes, you will," she said calmly.

"How? Tell me *how*."

"In the power of *His* might," said Mother. "Not your own, Keith. His resources are infinite, and they are all at the disposal of His ransomed ones."

Even now, with her mind worrying about how Keith felt and what he'd almost said, Sarah loved the sound of the big words Mother was saying. *Resources—infinite* (that's sort of like *everlasting*)—His *ransomed* ones. The words were so—so sort of splendid and majestic.

But Keith turned away and tramped out of the kitchen,

out of the house. The door closed with a thud. Then there was silence.

"I'll sweep that up," Mother said in her ordinary voice. "You'd better finish the lamps now."

Mother mixed the bread dough, and Sarah polished the last globe. They were one short now, and there was no new globe in the house. But on the top cabinet shelf there was an old one with an oval piece of glass missing. Mother boiled some thick paste and stuck a roundish piece of white canvas over the hole. By rights Keith should have had that lamp, but Mother told Sarah to carry it into the downstairs bedroom where she and Father slept.

Then the door opened, and Keith was back. He looked just ordinary again, smiling and calm.

"Mother, do you suppose I may kidnap—" he began.

But that instant the telephone bell rang, two longs and two short. The Scott ring. Mother went to answer it.

Keith tweaked Sarah's earlobe and grinned down at her.

They heard Mother say, "Oh? Well, how *good* of you, Mr. Slocum. . . . Oh, I'm *sure* he. . . Well! Is that so? . . . Wonderful! I'm sure he. . . Thank you. Care to talk to Keith himself?" Then she stared at the receiver a moment. "He's hung up," she announced.

But she had news. Exciting news. Mr. Slocum, their neighbor, had just come back from a cattle-buying trip to Alberta, and he'd brought back a cow pony for Keith.

"Not Masquerade!" exclaimed Keith.

"I think that's the name," agreed Mother. "Your former boss sent a message saying that the horse has been moping since you left. He's no earthly good to *them*, he says, so horse and master might as well be reunited. Compliments of the boss and riders of the C Bar P."

Keith's face was alight, and his voice shook. "Well, how do you like that?" he said.

Keith liked it all right, that was plain. And now he finished what he began asking before Mr. Slocum's call. He'd like to *kidnap* Sarah for a few hours, take her for a ride. He had meant for one of them to ride Wally and the other to take Hyacinth. Now he'd take Masquerade, of course.

"And I'd have Hyacinth! Goody! May I, Mother? May I, please?"

Mother looked at the unwashed dishes, and Sarah saw a *no* look beginning to gather in her eyes.

"We could promise to be back in half an hour, if you say so," Keith offered.

"No—" [*Whoosh* went Sarah's heart, down a toboggan slide. The next instant it was whizzing dizzily back up again, because this time *no* meant *yes!*] "Better make a day of it," decided Mother, just like that. "Run along, bundle up, Sarah. There, that's enough. Yes, yes, I mean it! No need to squeeze me in half! I'll pack a lunch for you two."

She did it while Keith rode to Slocums' to get Masquerade. Under Mother's directions Sarah had to put on two sweaters—two!—under Robbie's last year's jacket. And some bulky things under his overalls. Pants—on a girl! She looked like a very roly-poly gingerbread boy when she got through.

"Mother! I won't be able to *move!*" she protested.

She was almost too excited to think. A winter outing— with Keith—on a *Saturday!* And she could hardly wait to see Keith's cow pony.

When she did, she felt disappointed. He looked ordinary —tough and sort of flea-bitten and just plain ordinary. His coat was a dirty dusty brown in color. But when Sarah

came waddling out, Keith stood patting his neck and murmuring words, and Masquerade seemed to be whispering something right back at him.

"Over here, Sarah," called Keith. He didn't crack a smile at sight of her pants! "Masquerade," he said formally, "meet someone very special—the Prairie Princess. Shake hands with him, Sarah."

And Masquerade held out his right front hoof!

He was wearing his own special saddle too, with a brand-new rope coiled on the side.

"What's that for?" Sarah wanted to know.

"Cattle ropin', ma'am. Important equipment. No cowboy rides out without his rope. Got any calves need ropin', ma'am?"

"Ooh, Show me!" begged Sarah.

Keith laughed and said there was hardly room enough in the yard for any fancy roping. Besides, hadn't they planned to go riding? He left the rope where it was, though, because Sarah begged him to. It looked nifty there. But he said he hoped they wouldn't meet anyone on the way. People might think him a show-off.

Well, with a horse as smart as Masquerade, Sarah hoped they *would* meet people! No, she didn't either! She had never really had Keith to herself since he came home. Always there were grownups wanting to talk with him.

Mother came out with their packet of lunch done up in a flour sack (that was Keith's idea) and he knotted it to his saddle. Then he helped Sarah onto Hyacinth, and they were off. They headed west until they passed the Slocum farm. Then they swung north.

This Saturday morning ride was one of the nicest things that had happened to Sarah in all her whole life. Farmsteads were getting scarcer, because they were nearing the river, and pretty soon there was nothing around them but miles of snowy hills and black bushes and echoing quietness.

Sometimes they walked their horses, sometimes they trotted. The trotting helped to warm Sarah up, but she liked the walking best because that was when they talked.

Keith told her bits about all the years when he was away. It made Sarah feel grown-up—important. He told how he'd wanted and wanted to come back, but he'd been too ashamed to. Being away was worst at Christmastime, he said, but gradually he sort of got used to it. He got used to drifting through life, wasting it.

"But you're not wasting it anymore," Sarah said quickly.

"No. I hope not. But know something? Right now Stuart is twice the man I am. He accepted home discipline. I ran away from it."

Sarah wanted terribly to say something to comfort him. But—maybe he was right—in a way. It must be a sad way to feel though.

"Remember this, Sarah—remember it always," said Keith. "You can never live life over again. But what is left of mine I've given to God."

Sarah felt a prickle of something. Maybe Keith was thinking about her grumbling. She hadn't been "accepting home discipline" when she did that!

But then Keith cheered up suddenly. He told her funny stories and teased her. This road was pretty private, so he showed her some of the tricks he and Masquerade could do, and it was exciting. This was the road Father and the boys took to get wood; but instead of following it to the river flat, they turned west and then south, making a wide loop. Sarah was glad. She didn't want Robbie to know about her Saturday until afterward. Wouldn't he be surprised!

It was getting near 1 o'clock! Sarah and Keith found a heap of rocks on the south side of a bush. They ate their lunch in the warm sunshine there. But it was too cold to sit still for long, so they rode on again.

For Sarah, this was new country, rough and interesting. She could see farmhouses—Siddons' and Thatchers' and Heathes'—and the Braeburn school. But all of the buildings—and land looked unfamiliar because she was seeing them from the west. It was like looking at a map upside down.

"Hush!" said Keith suddenly, reining in Masquerade. "What was that? Whoa, Hyacinth."

The horses stood. There was nothing. No *special* sound—

Then it came—a bellow, cracking the silence and sort

of funneling along the fence-line trail they were following.

"Oh, that's Thatcher's bull, I guess. He's a mad one."

"Penned up, I hope!" said Keith sharply.

"Oh, sure. Well, *mostly* anyway," said Sarah. "He's a
mean one. Sometimes he does break through fences. But
he's valuable, and he wears a ring in his nose, and Stella
says you can lead him by it. Even she can! He just has to
behave."

That moment Sarah saw something drifting through the
trees—a horse! Hey, that was Louise Thatcher's Marmion!
And he wore a saddle. His bridle reins dangled, and they
kept catching on shrubs and tree branches.

For a moment Keith sat very still, staring at the horse.
"I feel uneasy," he said. "Think you can catch the horse,
Sarah?"

"Why, I guess, maybe—"

That moment the shattering bellow came funneling
along the tree-bound trail again. This time Keith raised
his voice excitedly.

"Catch him if you can, and snub him to a post. Then
follow me. But whatever you do, keep clear of trouble."

"What trouble?"

"Whatever it is. There's trouble ahead, or I miss my
guess!" And then he went rocketing away!

Catching Marmion wasn't awfully difficult, though he
snuffed a bit more than usual, as if he felt uneasy too.
Sarah managed to catch him and snub him to a fence
post. She had to slide off Hyacinth and crawl through the
barbed-wire fence; and being so stiff with heavy cloth-
ing, it wasn't easy. Then her snowy foot kept slipping
from the stirrup when she tried to climb back on Hyacinth. So it was a while before she rode on again.

About a quarter of a mile farther along, her way was barred by another fence. It had no gate. But Masquerade's tracks just stopped short—and began again on the other side. He must have jumped right over with Keith on his back. They'd been in an awful hurry. And no wonder!

In a clearing a little clump of poplars stood. Things were happening there—terrible things. Thatcher's bull was charging one of the poplars. Again and again! Each time his forehead rammed it, the tree shivered and shook. And clinging to one of the branches was what looked like a cougar at first—flattened and slender. It was Louise! She made no sound.

Sarah's mittened hands flew to her face. She wanted to shut out the sight. But she had to keep looking. She heard a sobbing, moaning sound, and it was coming from her own mouth. But still she couldn't help looking.

Keith had been trying to distract the bull and get him to follow Masquerade. It was no use. He just backed away a bit for another charge at the tree. Well, that minute the rope snaked out. It caught the bull's horns. And now the cow pony was hauling at the rope and pulling the bull right *to* the tree. And now Keith and Masquerade were doing a sort of ring-around-the rosy ride, round and round the tree clump. Each time the bull got tied up tighter! Now he wanted to go somewhere else. He bellowed. He raked the snow with his hooves. But he was caught.

Sarah laughed and cried to see it.

Keith rode under the tree and held up his arms, and Louise tumbled into them. Then they came galloping to the fence, and Keith lowered Louise near Sarah.

Safe.

Masquerade backed, took a run, and came sailing over the fence, and Keith slid off. For a minute all three just tried to catch their breath.

"Feel able to ride?" Keith asked Louise. "You take Hyacinth. We have your horse safe. You caught him, didn't you, Sarah? Up you get behind me, Princess."

Louise still couldn't say much, and Sarah couldn't blame her one little bit. She looked her thank-yous, and Sarah was proud to have her know how splendid Keith was!

Even when Louise was back on Marmion, they didn't leave her to ride alone. All three rode around to Thatchers' place. Louise's dad and her brother Crawford went for the bull as soon as they heard. But Mrs. Thatcher insisted that Sarah and Keith had to come indoors and have some of her fresh rolls. Sarah had milk with hers. The rest had coffee.

Louise was calm enough now to tell how she got into trouble with the bull. She hadn't known he was free. She'd heard him bellowing, but she hadn't thought anything of it. Marmion seemed to be limping, so she got down to examine his hoof—and suddenly out of the corner of her eye she saw the bull charging in terrible silence. Even then she would have been safe if she could have got back on Marmion. But the horse must have been startled too. He galloped away, so there was nothing for Louise to do but sprint to the nearest sizable tree. Fortunately there was one handy that was big enough to bear her weight.

Louise's face was still pale, but her eyes were the darkest blue that Sarah had ever seen.

"I prayed for help," she said simply. "But I'm afraid I didn't expect God to send a cowboy complete with trick pony and lasso! At first I simply couldn't *believe* it!"

"Blame it on Sarah," said Keith, smiling. "She insisted I had to take the rope with me today."

CHAPTER 4

Of Geese and Mrs. Gerrick

AND THEN IT WAS TIME to start for home.

Mrs. Thatcher came outdoors to stand in the wind with her apron pulled over her elbows, looking up at Keith. Her eyes filled with sudden tears.

"We, none of us, will ever be able to thank you enough for what you've done today," she said. "When I think of what might have happened to Louise—"

"Don't," said Keith earnestly. "It didn't happen. God sent us along just in time. It must have been God who made Sarah beg me to take the rope along."

"Well, then," said Louise's mother with a shaky laugh, "accept my thanks for humoring your little sister. And do come and see us soon, all of you."

"We will," called Keith and Sarah together. And then they rode away.

They didn't walk their horses this time. Darkness was coming fast. Keith usually watered and fed the cows if Father wasn't at home to do it. As for Sarah, she thought suddenly of the heap of shoes that had to be polished. Mother wouldn't have had time to do them. Besides—but this thought put a sparkle into her dark eyes—besides, she hoped to get home before Robbie. *Wouldn't* she have an adventure to tell!

As it happened, Masquerade and Hyacinth felt pretty

42

peppy. They went loping along side by side and sort of swept up the Scott lane at last. Keith took charge of Hyacinth then.

Sarah had trouble getting to the house. She was so stiff from the chill and from being stuffed into so many layers of clothes, and Ginger insisted on rolling and mewing on the snow at her feet and between her ankles, tangling her up.

"You! Ginger! Scat!" she scolded, laughing.

"Have a good time?" asked Mother a minute later. Then, "Sarah, child! Out you go! Sweep off your boots before coming indoors! My newly washed floor!"

Well, when you have an adventure story bubbling inside you, it's hard to think of things like snow on your boots.

When Sarah came back indoors she noticed the kitchen had its Saturday look and smell. Shining. Quiet. But bubbly too. Sarah sniffed. Soap. That was from the scrubbing. Supper must be roast pork and baked apples. And new bread, of course. The loaves formed a crackling row on the kitchen cabinet.

Sarah began shedding sweaters and socks, and all the while her tongue was running on about today's happenings.

"That animal!" said Mother disapprovingly. She never just plain said the word *bull*. She thought it wasn't ladylike. "The Thatchers should get rid of him."

"But he's valuable!" protested Sarah. "Mr. Thatcher's building a really strong corral for him. Stella said so. And—"

"Father's home." said Mother.

Sarah could hear Spencer barking as she pulled off Robbie's long woolen stockings. Her own came with them. Barefoot, she raced to the nearest window and looked out.

Outdoors it was dusky by now. You could see cow shapes moving near the trough, dipping their muzzles, and moving away a bit, then drinking again. The lantern hung from a nail at the well-house door. And now the teams came, each drawing a long load of felled trees. Father and the boys would probably unload the wood before supper because they would need one of the bobsleighs to go to church tomorrow.

"And who's going to polish the shoes?" said Mother.

"Me. In just a minute," said Sarah, hurrying to pull her stockings on again.

She was sitting in the corner on the floor of the kitchen with a heap of shoes around her when Father and the boys finally walked in. A lantern smell came trailing in with them. They'd taken quite a bit of time because of the unloading and the milking and getting acquainted with a new horse.

"Had yourself quite a day, did you, Princess?" said Father.

Sarah nodded, buffing away. Her grin was especially for Robbie. Usually his Saturdays were more exciting than hers. Not today!

He looked at the heap of black and brown shoes. "That's what you get for riding off," he said.

"Who cares? I guess I'll be through by the time you're washed."

And she was. Almost anyway. She slid into her chair just as Father finished carving the roast.

Supper was good, and the kitchen was cozy. Funny thing though. Little chills kept playing tag up and down Sarah's back, and the lamplight blurred and bobbed before her eyes. So she ate in silence mostly, listening to the others talking.

Keith announced that he'd had an idea today. Did Father know, was Herbie's farm for sale? Because, he'd sort of like to go into business for himself—raising cow ponies. Robbie and Stuart got excited over the idea.

"I intend to go on studying and reading, of course," said Keith, with a half smile at Sarah. "But it's high time I was making my own way—if I can."

"*We* have no doubt on that score, son," said Father quietly.

"But your health—" began Mother anxiously.

"I'm well. Besides, I wouldn't be far away. You can go on pampering your big son, I promise you," said Keith jokingly.

Father said that Mr. Gerrick was coming next week to saw the wood, so that would be a good time to ask about the farm. And Mother said if Mr. Gerrick was coming, that would be a good time to butcher the geese. Mrs. Gerrick had offered to help.

Usually that job got done in the fall; but because Sarah's parents spent almost a month in Ontario last fall, some chores got left. Lately the sassy brassy things had been penned in one corner of the chicken house. The chickens didn't like them there, and neither did Sarah, whose job it was to take out the eggs. They ganged up on her, hissing and honking and snapping at her, and their bills could really bruise one's legs.

She liked fluffy goslings in spring. And she didn't mind growing geese in the yard in summer, even if they messed it up a lot. But in winter she liked them best in a roaster, all brown and crackling. Better still, on her plate, with dressing and mashed potatoes and other vegetables.

Mmm. Besides, the feathers made lovely pillows, and the wing tips were dandy brushes for clearing the table of crumbs, or for sweeping the stairs. You could get into the corners so well with them. Last year's wings were practically worn down to the bone now.

It was time to clear the table and to rush through the remaining Saturday night chores. Father trimmed the boys' hair, and Mother trimmed his—over in the corner farthest from the cabinet. Robbie fed the calves. Sarah dried the dishes.

As always, Saturday night was singing time. Things weren't quite the same since Kathleen left. But Keith was here now, and he had a guitar and could do fancy chords and runs on it. Mother played the organ. Tonight, because supper had been a bit late and because the long hours outdoors had made them sleepy, they cut the singing short. Then Sarah got first turn at the round tub in the kitchen, and she scampered up to bed.

Next morning, Keith and Stuart rode to church in the one-horse sleigh. This was because Susan's ma had invited all the young people of the church to her home for the afternoon. Sarah's big brothers wouldn't be home for dinner or supper. The rest of them rode in the bobsleigh as usual. Their backs were turned toward the wind, but they crowded close as possible for warmth. It was a cold morning.

Sarah and Robbie were stamping their feet under the buffalo robe to keep them warm. Sarah thought maybe she'd get to go to Gerricks' too. Mother said that if Susan asked her, and if Mrs. Gerrick said she might, well then, they'd see! There'd be a big dinner—and hours of singing—and maybe some coasting. It would be fun.

Sunday school came—and went. Susan sat right next

to Sarah, but she didn't say a word about inviting Sarah. After the service Sarah stood beside Susan in the cloakroom. They talked about things—different things. Not a word about this afternoon. Mrs. Gerrick was in a big hurry to get home today. She called, and Susan went running to hop into the double-seated sleigh, and the Gerricks drove away.

Sarah sighed and walked slowly to where Father and Robbie waited. They had shifted the bench and the robes around so the wind was at their backs again. Father sat on the edge of the box, whistling hymn tunes on the way home. Sarah and Robbie stamped their feet in time to the whistling. But they had their noses buried in their collars, and no one said much all the way home.

It wasn't as if Sarah didn't have things to *do* at home. She had two letters to answer—Kathleen's and Linda's. She told school news and about Louise Thatcher's rescue! It was exciting to write about.

Then it was choring time—and suppertime—and getting-ready-for-church-again time. Susan came to sit beside Sarah in church. Almost immediately she fell asleep, and her head toppled onto Sarah's shoulder and *stayed* there. Susan's ma stared at Sarah and made a jabbing motion with her elbow. Sarah was supposed to awaken her. She pretended not to see, though she didn't know if this was a naughty thing to do or not. Father wouldn't think it *very* naughty, she thought.

Most likely Susan had had to work hard all afternoon while helping her ma to feed about 30 people besides the family. She was so *capable* for 10 years old. That's what her ma always said.

On Thursday, goose-butchering day, Mrs. Gerrick talked a lot about that again. Sarah sometimes thought it would be easier to be friends with Susan if Susan's ma didn't always *brag* about her so.

This day after school Sarah and Robbie could hear from quite a distance what was going on at home. Oh, not the goose cleaning, of course, but the wood-sawing. Days were getting longer, but today was foggy. You couldn't see much, but sound traveled far. From a mile away you could hear the Fordson engine stuttering—and the wood being cut. The wood-cutting had a complaining, questioning sound.

W-h-a-a-a-a-a-t? *W-h-a-a-a-a-a-t?* That's the way the thicker logs sounded.

The *whats* grew shorter as the logs grew thinner, and finally sounded like *whut-whut-whut?*

Through the fog, when they came to a stop near the bush, they could see Father and Mr. Gerrick carrying logs and holding them up to the whizzing, round blade. And they heard the *clunk-clunk* as Keith tossed the pieces onto the growing pile. Green poplar has an exciting smell, sort of bitter and sweet. But the kitchen—well! That smelled mostly of steam and feathers and fat.

Mother sat plucking the breast feathers off the second to last goose. A towel was spread across her lap, and the headless goose lay on the towel. She grasped handfuls of down. *Rrutch-rrutch*—off they came, and she dropped them into a tall cardboard box beside her. Bits of down floated around though. Some clung to Mother's hair, to the coats in the corner of the room, and to the cabinet.

When Mother had finished plucking the breast feathers, Susan's ma took the goose from her and dunked it into the boiler on the stove. Not too long because the flesh mustn't cook, but the moist heat loosened the large feathers.

The table was heaped with naked geese. It didn't look as if supper would be ready soon, and Sarah was *hungry*. Without bothering Mother, she peeked into the pantry. Today's lunch hadn't seemed *nearly* enough.

There were mashed potatoes and some pieces of sausage. You had to ask about sausage. Most likely Mother would say yes, but Sarah didn't feel like interrupting. You could help yourself to bread and potatoes any old time. With the back of a spoon she spread potatoes over a half slice of brown bread, and peppered and salted it. Chewing, she scampered up to change her dress.

She almost choked on the bread though when Mrs. Gerrick's voice came drifting up the stairs.

"Where has Sarah disappeared to? Doesn't she help you? She's older than my Susan, and Susan saves many steps for me."

"So does Sarah for me," said Mother calmly.

"That Susan's a wonder, if I do say so, as I shouldn't!" bragged Mrs. Gerrick. "No sooner at home, than she's out of her school things and comes to ask what she can do to help me. Never wastes her time over books the way some children I see."

And Sarah thought, *Why doesn't Mother say something?*

She could have said that Sarah did that too. She did the very same as Susan—sometimes. Tonight she couldn't because now it would seem as if she was *copying*. In fact, she didn't feel like going down at all today.

"Sarah?" called Mother. She still sounded calm though. "Keith watered the cows a while ago."

"Coming, Mother," said Sarah.

"Well, about time!" said Mrs. Gerrick with a little laugh when Sarah came skimming down the stairs. "You'll

have to remember, Sarah. You're your mother's kitchen helper now."

"Yes, Mrs. Gerrick," said Sarah politely, because Mother would expect her to.

She got into her milking outfit in a hurry and grabbed the milk pails. She was out of the house as fast as she could go, but then she stood still to take one deep breath and to let it out slowly again.

Why was it, she wondered—Robbie often said, "Well, it's about time!" to her. And she never minded. Well, hardly ever. But if Susan's *ma* said it, it made her sweater collar feel choky. Every time.

The milk pails clanked on her arm as she ran across the yard. Spencer bounded happily beside her, and Ginger was waiting for her at the barn. A shove of her elbow sent the door to one side, its casters squeaking along the track.

"Well, who's in a rush tonight?" said Stuart, who was busily brushing Hyacinth. They had just gotten back from Blakely.

"It's that Mrs. Gerrick!" said Sarah. "She—just about makes me *explode.* She's so—so nosy."

"Now—now—" he warned. But he smiled in sympathy. She guessed they all felt pretty much alike about Kathleen's mother-in-law. Mother always excused her, sort of, by saying she was a very *well-meaning* woman. But if you *hurt* people, you *hurt* them, whether you meant to or not!

Sarah sighed, and then she forgot about Mrs. Gerrick. For the time being, anyway.

As always, Speckles sat on Brindle's back. Her newest egg, still warm, was nestled in Sarah's pocket. Ginger came to sit beside Sarah's stool expectantly. If Sarah pretended not to notice, she'd soon feel the pat of a paw on her knee. If she sent a stream of milk at the cat, he took it with a hissing sound, hardly wasting a single drop! Then he blinked at her, and washed his face—and waited for another jet of milk.

Supper that evening wasn't so bad. In fact, *supper* was delicious. But the talk wasn't as worrisome as Sarah had expected, because Mrs. Gerrick wasn't leading it. Mr. Gerrick and Father and Keith did most of the talking. All about Herbie's farm—and about Keith's idea of turning it into a horse ranch. Could he make it pay? That was the question. He thought he'd do some grain farming, but mostly he'd like to handle horses. And he thought he knew enough ranchers who were always looking for good riding stock.

"Thinking of settling down?" said Mrs. Gerrick. "Too bad I don't have a daughter to offer you. My Susan's a bit young." She laughed. "But Braeburn surely has some pretty girls, as you must have noticed last Sunday. And I'm sure one of them could be persuaded to assist you in starting a home of your own. That was a fine testimony you gave last Sunday night. A very fine testimony."

And it was. Keith had told them at home how he became a Christian. But until last Sunday night he'd never up and said so in church. But then he did. A lot of people were wiping their eyes and blowing their noses softly when he got through.

But somehow—the way Susan's ma talked about it— why, it sounded as if she thought Keith had done it so the girls could see what a fine husband he would make!

"Thank you, Mrs. Gerrick," said Keith gravely.

Then Father changed the subject.

After supper, and after the dishes were done, Sarah escaped to the parlor. She curled up in the large rocker. The room was warm, and one didn't need a lamp here.

Firelight came through the mica doors, flickering over the furniture. Just at first though, you couldn't see. That was why, when Father came in a few minutes later, he almost sat down on Sarah.

"Hey, I'm here!" she protested. Then she scrambled up. "But you can have the rocker, Father."

"Thanks. Can't have you more thoroughly squashed and flattened than you are already," he said.

"Squashed? Flattened? What do you mean, Father?" Sarah asked slyly.

Because, she knew. And he knew that she knew. And she knew that he knew that she knew.

He only chuckled and pulled her onto his lap.

"I'm sort of big for lap-sitting. Going on 11."

"Dreadful!" he agreed. "I don't suppose Susan ever dreams of doing this."

She could feel him shiver with silent laughter, and she giggled a bit too. Then she whispered into his ear,

"God sure did a good job of choosing Mother for us, didn't He?"

"Amen," said Father.

And Susan thought, *Having a mother who not only "means" to be kind but who "is" kind—that's the richest you can be.*

CHAPTER 5

Shadow on Groundhog Day

WINTER DAYS just inched along, it seemed to Sarah. Days were gray and white mostly, with snow tumbling down day after day, and the sleigh tracks on the road piling higher and higher. The fence posts simply got *drowned* in the white stuff. Fields looked like tossing oceans of white water. Overhead the sky was a shallow gray bowl, turned upside down. Whenever the sun came out, the sky turned a pale powder blue. But the dazzling fields and bushes hurt your eyes then.

In fact, there seemed to be something wrong with Sarah's eyes on the way home from school this Friday. She felt cross as two sticks besides—for no reason! That was the silly thing. Her throat felt like sandpaper, and her hands were sweating in the woolen mitts. She wished her eyes would stop hurting, and that Robbie would stop whistling through his teeth. Keith could whistle tunes through his teeth, and ever since he came home Robbie had to keep practicing. Usually she didn't mind.

Wally had turned east for the final half mile of the way. But Father was ahead of them on the trail, just plodding along. The bobsled he drove was loaded with ice blocks, so Sarah knew he'd been to the river today. He sat on the ice, with only the buffalo robe between him and it. A pretty chilly perch. So why didn't he hurry a bit more?

Robbie didn't think it would pay to pass him, the snow being so deep and all, so Wally had to slow to a walk too.

"Why are you *fussing* like this?" Robbie said to Sarah.

"I'm *not* fussing."

"Well, whining then. It's not as if it's dreadfully cold today, or anything."

"I'm not whining either," protested Sarah. Her voice did have this funny quavering sound though.

One good thing, days were getting longer bit by bit. But milking Brindle was a dreadful chore tonight. And supper—scalloped potatoes, and baked sausage, and applesauce—all Sarah's favorites ordinarily—tasted like nothing at all tonight. The potatoes were like the paste Mother used last summer to paper the parlor! Sarah said so in a grumbling undertone.

Mother had sharp ears. "Sarah Scott!" she exclaimed, scandalized. "Now finish your supper. And no more grumbling!"

"I'm just not hungry, I guess," said Sarah.

"Do you think she's coming down with something, Mother?" asked Father.

"She has a slight cold. You'll have to go to bed early," decided Mother.

Next morning Sarah felt fine, so Father asked Mother if he might borrow the princess to help outdoors. The dry wood needed to be stacked in the woodshed, and the newly sawn wood stacked in its place outdoors for curing next summer. This was a daylong job for everyone.

Father had fastened a box to the little sled, and Robbie and Sarah used that to haul wood. With each load they brought more snow into the shed, but nobody minded. They pulled the sled right over the sill. The more snow there was, the easier it was to pull their loads in.

On a long table along the north wall lay all the iced meat—beef and chickens and geese. You froze them, and then you dunked each piece or fowl into water several times till a thick coat of ice formed. It kept the meat fresh and tasty as long as the cold weather lasted. So that was one handy use for the woodshed.

But most of the space was used for wood. The place got to smelling woodier and woodier as Sarah and Robbie stacked the split stuff as high as the rafters. They fooled around a lot too, laughing like anything at the way Sarah's voice was getting more and more quavery. Outdoors, Father, with Keith and Stuart's help, was making a neat pile of the newly sawn wood. A fortification, Robbie named it. But Sarah thought it would make a dandy playhouse next summer.

This was a strange day, she found. Sweating hot or shivering cold—her body couldn't make up its mind what to be! Mother was about twice as busy as usual today. She was melting ice chunks for Monday's wash, besides doing the other indoor Saturday jobs. So she never thought to feel Sarah's forehead.

"I *know* you've worked hard," she said at 5 o'clock. "But so has everyone else. You have only one cow to milk. The sooner you begin, the sooner you'll finish."

That's one of the things grown-ups like to say. And most of the time it's true. But—

The path to the barn seemed an immense distance today. Spencer came to jump on her—and they rolled in the snow together. He was up in a flash. When she floundered for a while, a funny whine came to his throat. She laughed her queer hoarse laugh, and he whined anxiously again. Then he paced slowly beside her, and walking was a bit easier because she could hold onto him.

Afterward she seemed to remember leaning against the barn door, and moving past Masquerade's stall and leaning against the post where his saddle hung—and moving to the cow stanchions—and holding on to the iron hook with both hands— She seemed to remember getting the milking stool and sitting down on it beside Brindle. But that was all. She had forgotten to bring any milk pails, but she never noticed.

She heard from the others what happened next. How Spencer almost barked his head off—such whining barks that Father came running because he knew something serious must have happened. How Robbie, in the hayloft, heard the same bark and jumped into the haymow and sprained his ankle, so he had to hobble for days. How Father, looking as pale as putty, carried her to the house.

No one was too busy now. Nothing else mattered. Sarah was sick, very sick. They told her about it later, taking turns at repeating it over and over. She was sorry she couldn't remember anything. Imagine! All that fuss made over her!

For days Sarah knew no one. She was delirious and talked a lot, but nobody could understand her because she was so hoarse. The doctor came from Paxton. She had a severe case of the flu, he said—nothing more. And he *didn't* think that stacking the wood on Saturday had done any harm, though it probably brought the whole thing to a head faster.

Gradually Sarah began noticing things again. Slow creeping nights—mornings tiptoeing in finally—Mother raising her hot head to hold a cup of lemonade to her cracked lips—Father just sitting beside her, holding her hands or rubbing her back gently—Robbie peering in with an awed look, then ducking out—doors slamming—the clock tick-tocking—an orange locomotive chugging over her from toe to head and peering down at her face. Then the cowcatcher turned into whiskers, and the locomotive was Ginger! Sarah giggled—and then cried a bit because the giggle hurt her throat.

She longed for Spencer, and they told her that he lay as close to the door as possible and kept watching for her. But they couldn't drag him in. He never came indoors except in an emergency—mostly during a thunderstorm. But Sarah remembered the blizzard last fall when he saved Robbie's life. He came in that time.

She was well enough now to smell the goose grease that Mother rubbed and rubbed into her chest and throat.

"Hush," said Mother. "It's not a disagreeable smell. Rather like a good fresh roast."

"But who wants bed to smell like a roast?" croaked Sarah crossly.

Father, who was watching from the doorway, laughed suddenly. "You'll do. You're getting well. We'll soon have our spunky, lively little princess about again."

"Please, God," whispered Mother.

Sarah was surprised and touched to see sudden tears in Mother's eyes. Later, Robbie told her that Father said that Mother had blamed herself for making Sarah milk Brindle that day.

But it wasn't her fault! She simply didn't *know!*

Sarah tried to tell her mother so, but in the middle of groping for the words, she fell into a deep sleep. When she awoke next morning she was almost well. Her cough lingered a day or two longer, so Sarah had to linger in bed too.

Everyone tried to amuse her. Mother, patching Robbie's overalls beside her bed, told stories of when she was a girl in Ontario. Father carried the rocker—with Sarah in it—into the kitchen. He brought in the harness that needed mending too, and worked where she could watch him and sniff the leather and tar smells. Keith showed her how to do some fancy braiding with wool and leather. In the evenings Stuart taught her some tricky math puzzles—real nifty ones—and Robbie brought her library books to read. He also brought her some assignments from Teacher, so she wouldn't lose so much time.

Mother cooked special dishes for her—all the things she liked especially well. It wasn't really necessary though. Now that the flu was over and the sore throat gone, Sarah was hungrier than she had been in all her life!

There was one happening that frightened Sarah for a minute. Tuesday morning, ten days after she took sick, she got up. She was tottery and clung to chairs and walls when she walked anywhere. But that wasn't the startling thing. She combed her hair—and handfuls of it came loose. Simply handfuls! It felt dead and dry as hay. She thought of old Mrs. Parsons over near Blakely who always wore a cap. People said that was because she was *bald*. And now— And now—

"Sarah!" exclaimed Mother at sight of her stupefied face. "What ever—" Then she noticed the brush all clogged with dead hair, and she spoke comfortingly. "That's what often happens to people who have had a high fever, Sarah. Your hair is sure to grow back again. Probably thicker than ever."

Sarah's breath left with a relieved *whoosh*. It would have been dreadful for a girl going-on-11 to have to wear a little black lace cap all her life long!

Her head felt strangely light the first time she went back to school. And of course she couldn't help looking a bit strange too. But was that any reason why Susan should *laugh* at her?

"You look funny, sort of," she giggled. "And Sarah Scott! Right this minute you have a big blob of hair crawling across your back. Ugh! Take it away! Take it away!"

The big girls were kinder. They shook their heads in sympathy and said she must have been *really* sick. And look at all the tiny fuzz beginning to grow along her hairline. They thought it was going to come out curly. They really did! All of them had relatives or friends or someone they knew about who had had this happen to them. Imagine! No more knobby curling rags when your hair was supposed to look particularly nice, like for Kathleen's wedding last fall.

Sarah couldn't help repeating what they had said about her hair to Susan.

"But curly hair's an awful bother to comb. You can't keep it neat," said Susan, and she patted her own neat blonde hair in a satisfied way.

Somehow Sarah felt like a kitten—an innocent little kitten—who expected to be petted, but whose fur got stroked the wrong way.

Then there was this thing about the Irish play.

Most Braeburn pupils were about as Irish as they were Scottish. And a former Braeburn farmer, Mr. McDonnell, had offered a $5 prize to the pupil who would write the best Irish play. All this had happened while Sarah was sick, and Robbie hadn't said a word to her about it. Now Susan told her that *she* had written a play.

Susan. Why, she had no imagination at all. She ought to know that! But when Sarah mentioned it—just kindly mentioned it—Susan had to go and turn all prickly and huffy. And before you knew it, the two friends weren't friends anymore.

The very next Monday, Groundhog Day, Sarah had to drive to school alone.

It started out to be a perfectly lovely day. Only Johnny Siddons would be worried about the sunshine. The last thing he wanted on Groundhog Day was to see the sun, because the old superstition said that if a groundhog sees his shadow on February 2, there's going to be another whole month of winter weather.

The Siddonses were sort of superstitious. Father said that was the Irish in them. (Hoo! Irish! Father's mother was Irish too. But Sarah was glad she was Scottish, and that her name proved it.) But Johnny Siddons was the most superstitious of all. And it really was silly to worry about the groundhog. Out here winters almost always lasted longer than the 2nd of March!

Well, today was mild and sunny, but not too mild. The trail to school was pretty firm. Sarah was glad; she had worried about driving alone. Robbie was needed to help Father haul wheat to Blakely.

The thing about driving in winter was, if your horse blundered off the trail, or if you had to pass another sleigh, well, that was just too bad for you. *If* you weren't an experienced driver, the horse could sink into snow right to his belly. Floundering out of the trail and back onto it again was tricky. You could break your shafts, or at least upset the sleigh.

So Sarah was both afraid and terribly proud that Father thought she could do this thing alone. Keith harnessed and hitched Wally for her and made sure there was an oat sheaf for Wally to munch at school. Then he tucked the robe around Sarah's knees.

"You're sure you can manage, Princess? Perhaps I ought to drive you" he said a bit anxiously.

"She'll be all right," called Father from his seat high on his load of wheat. Robbie's load was right behind his, all ready to start, but they were giving her the right of way. "If you meet anyone today, let the other turn out of the trail. The drivers will excuse so young a driver, I know. Drive safely now."

"Y-yes, Father."

She hoped, oh, she hoped no one would be traveling between here and school. The wind was right; it came from behind. Wally went at his usual no-nonsense trot too. She soon left Father and Robbie far behind. Their teams would be walking most of the way to Blakely with their loads.

When she turned south, her heart skipped a beat. A

team! Coming toward her! But then she remembered Heathes' driveway was not so far away. Because she got there first, it was up to her to turn off the road so as to allow the other team to pass safely. The driver was Mr. Slocum. He waved his thanks when he passed, and Sarah could drive on again.

But, oh, *please*, not any more! It was pretty late now.

She was about a quarter of a mile from school when she saw another team topping the rise just ahead. Oh, dear! Now there was no driveway handy. So, remembering Father's instructions, she called Wally to stop and just sat there waiting. But the other team was hauling a load of wheat. And the rules say that if your sleigh has the lighter load, it's up to you to turn out. Everybody knows that.

The other team came to a stop too, right in the middle of the road. It was embarrassing.

Then Sarah breathed a sigh of relief. The other driver hopped briskly down, and she recognized Mr. Thatcher. Nobody had to be embarrassed in front of him! He came running, greeted her cheerfully, and took hold of Wally's bridle. He led the horse step by step—off the trail, past the other team with its load, and safely back onto the trail again. Then he waved his hands at Sarah and hopped back onto his load. So that was safely over, and Sarah wasn't even late that morning.

The Gerrick sleigh reached the school yard just ahead of Sarah. If she and Susan still were friends, maybe Chuckie or Bertie would unhitch Wally— Well, maybe they didn't know about the quarrel. Chuckie came running.

"Take him for you," he said matter-of-factly.

Susan even waited a bit so she and Sarah walked up the porch steps together. But—it's funny. When you're good friends you don't have to choose words. They come by themselves, and mostly they're the right ones. When things go wrong, you think and think, but no words come tumbling into your mind and onto your tongue. Unless they're hot and angry words.

In the coatroom Susan looked past Sarah, and Sarah looked past Susan. They placed their lunch pails side by side, as usual, but they didn't talk.

The big girls were chattering—Grace Millar and Violetta Siddons and the rest. The main topic was the St. Valentine's Day dance next week. Braeburn school always had one each year. Not the *church crowd*, of course. Violetta and Grace felt very sorry for the *church crowd* who never could do any fun things!

It didn't bother Sarah—much. The Scotts were *church crowd*. Look at the coasting and all! Not have fun! She knew better. But today she couldn't share the joke with Susan. That was an odd feeling.

About 11 o'clock the weather changed. The wind rose suddenly and slammed around the school. The furnace turned balky, so the room filled with smoke. That was because of the gusts of wind blowing suddenly down the chimney. And then the storm came roaring down—

The day didn't actually turn much colder, and the sky still hadn't clouded over. You could faintly see a blob of yellow overhead. But the air was filled with this powdery snow that just sifted down from every direction, and you couldn't see 10 feet ahead of you outdoors.

Sarah's heart had begun to do fluttery things. She ate her lunch slowly at noon, her eyes turning to the bleary sky every few bites. If only Robbie were here! Boys who dashed out to feed their horses, stumbled back in, gasping and puffing, all plastered with snow. The wind was doing funny things, they reported. There were the queerest drifts piling up here and there. Chuckie Gerrick had offered to tend to Wally, which was one good thing. But he wouldn't be able to drive him home for Sarah. So whatever would she do?

No one played outdoors today. Most of the pupils crowded the basement. They chinned themselves on the crosspieces. They took long jumps down the stairs. Some of the big girls and boys began playing trick games, like Magic Broomstick. Susan, Sarah noticed, was playing singing games with the beginners:

> Little Annie sewing in her little housie,
> No one comes to see her except her little mousie. . . .

Baby stuff!

And the wind grew worse and worse.

About 1:30 Mr. Gerrick phoned. He was chairman of the board of trustees, and he thought the pupils should be dismissed—whoever wished to go home early. Anyway, his children had better start for home immediately.

So Chuckie wouldn't even be here to hitch Wally for Sarah.

If she and Susan were friends, she might go to Gerricks for the night. She couldn't phone home. Teacher tried, and there was no answer. That line seemed to be tangled again, the way it was during the October blizzard last fall.

All the other pupils were tugging on their coats and tying scarfs over their faces, right up to their eyes. Sarah stood in the coatroom, feeling helpless and unhappy. Then the outer door slammed open. She heard a breathless voice asking.

"Is Sarah Scott still here?"

The snowy collar was thrown back. Keith's head

emerged—Keith's smile. Now everything would be all right again.

"You came for me!" she squealed.

"Of course. Did you think we wouldn't? We Scotts couldn't afford to do without you, now could we?"

"Oh, neither could Braeburn," said Grace Millar fervently. "Here, Sarah, let me tie that scarf for you. May I, dear?" But she really was looking at Keith.

Violetta buckled on Sarah's overshoes. And Grace handed her her lunch pail, patting her cheek, hoping she'd have a safe trip.

"But of course you will—with such a marvelous protector," she added.

Sarah didn't say a word until Keith had tucked her into the sleigh. He had shaken out the robes as well as he could, but they were snowy still, of course. The stuff came tumbling down so. Masquerade was tied to the rear of the cutter—which he didn't like at all. Keith got in beside Sarah and picked up the reins.

"You all set?"

She pushed the scarf aside for a bit. "They don't *usually* call me dear and help me dress—as if I was a baby," she said, displeased.

Keith shouted with laughter. "That's my spunky sister!" he said. "Giddap there, Wally."

CHAPTER 6
A Goodwill Ambassador

THE WIND WAS the strangest part of that strange ride home. It had a swishing howling sound, far off, and yet very close. But the snow was *everywhere*.

Sarah's scarf was tied so that she had a tiny breathing hole. But even so she shrank back behind Keith's right shoulder, because otherwise the air just seemed too thick to breathe. Looking out wasn't much use anyway. Even Keith seemed to be giving Wally his head. Masquerade might not like being tied behind, with nothing to do but follow; but Wally knew the road best, and he had a lot of horse sense.

He wasn't the fastest trotter, and he was sort of awkward-looking and stodgy. But he had good horse sense. That's what Keith and Sarah were counting on today.

Twice Keith stopped the cutter, climbed out, and waded into the snow to make sure that Wally was sure of his landmarks. And he was.

If you passed close enough to a farmstead you might see the jutting peak of a barn looming out of the whiteness high overhead—or perhaps the round blur that was the folded windmill head. For just a minute. Then it disappeared, and you were shut up again in this whirling cold whiteness.

Finally Wally stood. He just stood, hanging his head and heaving his flanks.

"Well, what do you know?" said Keith. "We're home. Sarah, we're home!"

That minute the curtain of snow blew aside a bit, and Sarah could dimly see a chimney sticking up out of the general nothingness. And that minute too, she heard Spencer barking somewhere—in the barn probably. He must have recognized Wally. He was welcoming them but didn't bother coming out right now!

Sarah couldn't blame him. It's a funny thing though. When you've been driving in a snowstorm, you can't *wait* to get where you are going. You just ache to be out of it. But then you arrive, and for just a minute you wish you didn't have to stir, because getting out of the sleigh and wading through the storm is a cold and shivery thing to do.

This time Sarah didn't have to do any wading. Keith left the horses where they were. They wouldn't run away! He simply picked her up and plunged through the drifts and never stopped until he could lower her onto the snowy porch. He was gasping for breath, but he plunged back into the snowstorm again to take care of the horses.

In the kitchen Sarah shook out her coat and scarf. Blobs of snow flew in all directions, but Mother didn't reprimand her at all.

"Sweep it up before it melts" was all she said.

And she went on trying to see through a tiny spot of clear glass in the east window. You couldn't see anything out there!

"I only hope all of them come back safely," she said with a sigh.

But then she began making supper—beefsteak pie—

and Sarah got to help pound the steaks. Soon the kitchen
had a rich supper smell. It was warm, and it was snug.
But it had a lonesome feeling until Robbie and Keith,
Stuart and Father all came tromping in to shake the snow
off *their* coats and mackinaws and to empty their buckled
overshoes. The linoleum was wet and slithery with the
stuff. So Robbie got busy with dustpan and broom, and
Sarah followed him with a basin and cloth.

A home is the snuggest place when there's a storm
blowing. That's what Sarah Scott thought that night.

Because of the flu and the storm, she got excused from
milking, though she couldn't get out of drying dishes. But
afterward Mother sat near the center table in the parlor,
darning socks. And Father sat in the rocker, reading
Masterman Ready aloud. Stuart was helping Keith with
some algebra problems at the kitchen table. But Robbie
and Sarah listened to Father, even though they were
making funny shadow pictures on the wall at the same
time.

Masterman Ready was a lot like *Swiss Family Robinson*,
thought Sarah. But it sounded more *real*. In *Swiss Family*
all their wishes came true so easily. They were all so
smart, and they built things so fast, and they could tame
the wildest animals—things like that.

"But Susan likes Swiss Family Robinson best," said
Sarah, giggling. "Except, she doesn't think a man ought
to *cry* so much."

"Huh?" said Robbie, staring in a puzzled way. "Mr.
Robinson? He doesn't."

"Sure." Sarah's eyes sparkled with mischief. "On practically every page! Don't you remember? It says things
like, ' "It's time for us to go, boys," I cried.' Or, ' "Avast
there," I cried.' "

"But *that's* not the same— *That* doesn't mean—"

Sarah giggled again. "I know. But Susan thought it did. She hasn't any imagination! Not a smidgen."

"She has many lovely qualities," said Mother quietly.

"But she *doesn't* have *any imagination*," insisted Sarah. "And she's going to look just plain silly, trying to write an Irish play."

"Hush, Sarah. No one hearing you would know you are speaking about a friend."

Friend. Ho-hum.

"Listen to that wind!" said Father as he laid *Masterman Ready* aside and reached for the big Bible.

By morning the storm had spent itself. There was this egg-white frosting on every bush and building, and monster snowdrifts here and there. Because the roads were blown over, Father hitched Prince and Captain to a bobsleigh and drove ahead of the cutter all the way to school, to break the trail for Robbie and Sarah.

A surprise waited for Sarah at school. The big girls were as friendly as they had been last night when Keith walked in. They even invited her into the coatroom at recess because they had an important question to ask. Well! They clustered around her as if she was the queen bee of a hive or something.

"We have the most *wonderful idea*," began Grace. "Usually Braeburn has this St. Valentine's dance every year. But it doesn't seem exactly fair. I mean, the school belongs to the whole district, but the church crowd can't *go* to dances—"

"We don't want to. We don't need to," said Sarah. "We do have a lot of fun things to do together."

"Of course you do," said Grace soothingly.

"What Grace means," volunteered Violetta, "is that we

thought it would be nice to have things different. Teacher likes the idea very much, and she thought it wouldn't hurt to find *out*, and—and—you having a couple of big brothers, and all—"

"Oh, Vi, you goose!" said Grace. "We still haven't told Sarah what it's all *about*."

So they told her. Really it was a question she was supposed to pass on to the "church crowd" young people through Stuart—because he was the president this year. If there'd be a party this year instead of a dance, would the "church crowd" come to it?

It was all very mysterious and secret. That is, here she was with all the big girls, and both doors of the hall closed. So when they let Sarah go—she was to be their goodwill ambassador, they said!—Well, when they let her go, there stood Susan alone in the hall outside the door, looking left out. There was no *goodwill-ambassador* look on her chubby face.

For a tiny minute Sarah felt sorry for her. But— Well, it was fun to pretend she had an important secret mission, and you don't go and blab to anybody about a secret mission—especially not to a friend who *isn't* a friend anymore.

Sarah spoke to Stuart and Keith at home—and they spoke to the others at church—and Sarah took a message back on Monday. The answer was yes—*provided*. They would like to share in providing the refreshments and in planning the games, and there must be no drinks stronger than coffee served!

Grace said that was perfectly all right. Grant and Teacher would be there, and her brother was a pretty good one to keep order.

The big girls kept right on being nice to Sarah—right up to the day of the party!

The decorations for the grown-up Valentine party were up all day, and during the last school period the school pupils had their own party with cake and lemonade and a Valentine Box. Robbie, who was the only grade-eight boy in school, was postman. He almost got tired of calling Sarah's name! There even were a few store-bought ones— from the big girls! And anyway, she got more valentines than Susan did.

But there was none from Susan—and Susan got none from her.

Sarah clutched her heap of valentines in mittened hands as she ran toward the sleigh. Susan stood at the bottom of the porch steps, waiting for her.

"*I* wouldn't let the big girls make a fool of me," she said, lifting her chin. "That's what they're doing to you, Sarah Scott. That's what my mother says. She says that the whole valentine party idea is just a way of getting your brother Keith here, because they're crazy, clean crazy, over him. That's what my ma says."

Sarah's scalp prickled because she'd had the same idea. What's more, Stuart must have had it too. Just the other night she saw him lean back after supper, his hands clasped behind his head and a tiny smile on his face. He said to Keith, "I suppose you are aware that there are ulterior motives behind the whole party scheme? My handsome big brother seems to have set feminine hearts aflutter and feminine tongues atwitter."

Keith laughed and tossed a glove in Stuart's face. So Stuart jumped up and they tussled in fun for a bit. Then they went out to do the night chores together.

So—it was true. *Maybe. But* Susan and her ma had no business talking about Keith like that!

Just then Robbie whistled impatiently through his

teeth. He and Wally were waiting to start home. Sarah looked past Susan at the gleaming field of snow. Peaceful. But there was a storm in Sarah's heart.

She mustn't let Susan notice. "It's going to be a *lovely* evening for a party," she said, and she ran toward the sleigh.

Everybody said later that the party was a success. Teacher told Sarah how much everyone had enjoyed the Irish skit Keith did. When she asked him about it at home, he did some *impersonations* for her—that's what he called them. He said there used to be an Irish couple cooking for the C Bar P ranch—the funniest characters. They must have been. Sarah laughed until she cried, just listening to Keith.

That night Sarah got the most tremendous idea—and the more she thought about it, the more she liked it. *She* would write an Irish play. She could, with Keith to help. All the plays that were any good were going to be presented at a program on St. Patrick's Day in March. And maybe, just maybe, Mr. McDonnell was going to be there in person. He'd written that he might be.

When Sarah spoke to Teacher about her idea, Mrs. Millar looked interested, but sober too.

"It wouldn't qualify for the prize, you know."

"It wouldn't?"

"I'm afraid not. Contest entries are to be independent work."

"Well, would it qualify for the program though?" said Sarah anxiously.

"I don't see why not. There's no harm in trying." And she smiled at Sarah's eagerness.

This was the most exciting thing that had happened to her, thought Sarah on the way home. Well, maybe not the very most. Riding with Keith and watching him rescue Louise Thatcher from a bull—perhaps that was the most exciting of all. But that was over in a few minutes. This excitement would last and last!

"I thought you didn't care about the contest," said Robbie, slipping his right hand out of his mitt for a minute to grope for a leftover sandwich in his lunch pail. "You're always making jokes, sort of, about Susan and her play."

"Well, *Susan*. She's got no imagination."

Robbie tucked a frozen bite of sandwich in his cheek before retorting. "You've said that about 15 hundred times."

"Robbie Scott! That's an exaggeration."

The mouthful of sandwich kept him busy for a minute. "Know something, Sarah?" he said then. "You remind me of some poetry." And he began reciting in a loud singsong voice,

> There was a young lady of Niger
> Who smiled as she rode on a tiger—"

Sarah interrupted with a sniff. "*Niger* and *tiger* don't match. I mean, they don't rhyme."

"Go tell that to the man who wrote the limerick, whoever he was. Now you just listen:

" 'There was a young lady of Niger—' "

"You said that before," muttered Sarah grumpily.

" 'Who smiled as she rode on a tiger,' " continued Robbie, ignoring her.

" 'They returned from the ride
With the lady inside
And the smile on the face of the tiger.' "

"What's that supposed to mean?" said Sarah, fascinated in spite of herself.

"This: You're riding a dangerous beast—"

"Silly. What beast?"

"Jealousy, near as I can make it out."

"*Jealousy!* Me, jealous? Of who?"

"Of *whom*," he corrected her. Then he added, "Of Susan, of course."

"Susan! That's silly. That's just plain *stupid. Susan.* Why, she has no imag—"

"Ah-ah. There you go again. You better watch it. One of these days that beast is going to swallow you up. Got any sandwiches left?"

"Half," she said, handing over her pail. Then she said in sudden exasperation, "Robbie Scott, sometimes you make me *so mad—!*"

All the rest of the way they were silent. The whole world was alight with a rosy-mauve glow because the sun was setting. Terribly beautiful—and terribly sad somehow. Fields were shiny as satin, and trailing wisps of loose-flowing snow were skimming across the satin. It reminded her of Kathleen's wedding dress with the filmy veil over it. Suddenly Sarah was almost unbearably lonesome for her sister.

Then she thought of Susan, wishing they were friends again and wondering a bit drearily how the whole trouble began. Just *little* things. They weren't her fault—Sarah just *knew* they weren't. At least, *most* of them weren't. Everything was tangled and mixed though, and how would anyone ever get it all sorted?

When they came to the Heathe driveway, they saw a team coming from the north. It was Father driving Prince and Captain. He must have been down to the river again for ice or wood. At the corner, instead of swinging east toward home, he kept on coming. So Robbie turned Wally off the trail and waited.

Opposite them, Father pulled up his team.

"Had a letter from Toronto today—from Aunt Jane," he said. "It seems she hopes to come back to her home in the spring."

"To *farm?*"

"I couldn't say. But I'm to fill her icehouse with blocks. Tell Mother I'll be home as soon as possible," he added, and drove on.

Robbie looked worried and far from pleased. Aunt Jane and an icehouse sounded like one thing: dairy farming. And after the accident she'd had, that might mean a lot of neighborly assists—and a going-on-14 boy is awfully handy to send on neighborly errands. Well, if there was a job Robbie just loathed, it was milking.

But Sarah's heart was bumping against her ribs with excitement. Aunt Jane Bolton coming back! That might mean that Linda was coming back too!

Arriving at home, she jumped out of the cutter, pushed Spencer and his slobbery tongue aside, scooped up her lunch pail and schoolbag, and was ready to dash for the house. Then she saw the two-seater sleigh in the yard. Gerricks'! What was Susan's mother doing here today?

Her steps slowed to a sober walk. Susan's ma would think it unladylike for a 10-year-old girl to go scooting in. But that wasn't what restrained Sarah. She had a strange feeling suddenly that something unhappy was about to happen.

For a moment she stood on the porch looking over the yard. The mauve and rose light had faded to a pearly gray, and that was sad too. She took a deep breath of

cold air. Then she opened the door quietly and walked
into the kitchen quietly.

"Good evening, Mrs. Gerrick," she said.

Her heart was on her tongue half the time during supper—each time Mrs. Gerrick glanced her way. But nothing happened. Mrs. Gerrick talked to Father and Keith
mostly, and after supper she didn't stop to help with the
dishes. But Sarah didn't mind. She'd never been more
happy to hear the jingle of trace chains fading away than
she was tonight.

But after the dishes were done and after Sarah had finished her homework, and after she and Keith had planned
a couple of scenes for the play, Mother spoke suddenly.
"Sarah, bring a lamp, will you? I'd like your help in the
attic."

And there it was again—that half-frightened feeling.
Why was that?

"Be careful how you carry the light," cautioned Mother.
"I have my hands full."

And she did—about six bagfuls of goose down! They
were light, but bulky. For weeks they had been dangling
two by two over the washline, to get thoroughly aired of
any barn smells. Throughout all the snowstorms they dangled and spun out there! Some were old feathers that
Mother had washed to fluff out again.

The attic was a fascinating place of shadows and smells.
Robbie used it more often than anyone else, mostly because the stepladder rose from the boys' bedroom. All the
rafters were studded with hoarfrost now. It had a smell
of shoes and flour and mothballs. Sarah peered into trunks
and dusty drawers of old chiffoniers. Mother tucked the
last sack of feathers into a trunk, added a few mothballs,
and let the lid drop. Then she sat on it.

"Come here, Sarah," she said soberly then. "I'd like to talk to you."

She said Susan's ma had come here today to talk about Sarah. Susan was unhappy. Almost every night she cried herself to sleep because Sarah wouldn't play with her and was rude to her—

"That's a lie!"

"*Sarah!*" said Mother.

"Well, it isn't true!" muttered Sarah.

They looked unhappily at one another. The lamp was sitting on the floor, and it cast weird shadows on Mother's face, making her eyes look like deep caves with glinting fires deep inside each.

"Suppose you tell it your way," suggested Mother after a minute.

"There's nothing to tell," said Sarah helplessly. "Nothing important. Nothing—"

"Nothing *substantial?*"

Sarah nodded.

"Try anyway."

"It's just—well, Mrs. Gerrick always *brags* on her so. She thinks I don't work enough. You know the way she does. And Susan blabs everything—and her ma tells her what to say to me—"

"Like—?" suggested Mother.

"Well, Susan said her ma said I was letting the big girls make a fool of me. Because they're friendlier with me. She says—Mrs. Gerrick does—that it's only because they're crazy about Keith. And she says you're not a good manager, because you let me wear my best coat to school. And Susan says she's more Kathleen's sister than me, because her name is Gerrick now. And—" She stopped because she'd seen a smile flickering across Mother's face. If there was one thing Sarah didn't like, it was being laughed at!

"Sarah, Sarah," said Mother with a sigh. "Such *little* things!"

"But if they pile up and pile up, they're not little. They're a *big heap.*"

Mother sighed again. "That's your problem, Sarah. You let them pile up. I know you are warm and impulsive and friendly. But I also know that your big weakness is holding grudges—"

"*Mother!*" wailed Sarah.

"Remember last summer—your experience with Linda?"

"But that was before—before—"

"Before you became a Christian. Was that what you meant to say?"

Sarah nodded, looking down.

Mother did a rare thing. She placed her hands along Sarah's cheeks and stooped to kiss her.

"When you pray tonight, Sarah, ask the Lord to show you if you've been behaving as a Christian ought to toward Susan."

CHAPTER 7
Stuart Takes a Hand

SARAH DIDN'T EXACTLY PRAY about it. Because sometimes when you had what Father called a "difference of opinion" with someone—well, you might have a sort of feeling that God might not side with you. He might— and He might not. And just in case He didn't, you'd rather not find out.

So Sarah didn't pray about the quarrel. Anyway, every time she thought about Mrs. Gerrick she got this hot bone sticking in her throat. You can't say things to grown-ups. They're always supposed to be *right*. Well, was it *right* for Susan's ma to come here and tell Mother a string of— of *exaggerations?* But just because she was a grown-up, you weren't supposed to sass back. And the whole thing really was her fault, even more than Susan's!

Susan— Well, it was sort of pitiful the way she played mostly with the grade-one children now. Singing games. "Little Annie sewing—" And that other one that was just as monotonous and sounded almost as sing songy:

> Who's going around my stony well?
> No one but little Johnny Linger.
> Don't take any of my fat sheep!
> The more I want, the more I take,
> And out goes little Johnny Linger!

81

It was plain pitiful!

This evening Sarah just about made up her mind she was going to be kinder to Susan though. Not because of Mrs. Gerrick's visit, but because of Susan—and because of Kathleen and Herbie. Mother said Herbie would be dreadfully distressed if he knew. She pointed out that in many ways Susan had the same sort of simple goodness that Herbie had.

If Sarah thought of Herbie—and of Susan— If she forgot about the hateful "That's what my ma says" comments— Why, she even *liked* Susan. Sort of, anyway.

So tomorrow she would speak to Susan first thing. She'd say, "Let's be friends again." Maybe she'd better make a valentine to prove she meant it. There were bits of lace and ribbon and tissue paper left. And she had two ends of a shoebox left too, for cardboard. She wouldn't write anything very mushy on it. Just—well, just something to show that Sarah Naomi Scott didn't hold grudges.

Sarah fell asleep before she finished planning the belated valentine.

And next morning turned out to be fox-and-geese day at Braeburn!

These past weeks the sun had been getting stronger day by day. None of the snow had actually melted, but it was glazing over with an icy crust and packing down. And last night an even covering of clean white snow had fallen. The sun on the dazzling snow, and the mild wind just simply drove every other thought out of Sarah's mind.

The world was new—all new and clean—and Robbie and Sarah went sort of wild on the way to school. It was that kind of day.

The other Braeburnites felt the same way. Before Robbie and Sarah got there, they had begun tramping out the big fox-and-geese wheel with its many spokes. The hub was the home of the geese, but they wouldn't stay at home. They kept wandering away along the spokes, or paths, and that's when the wiley fox caught them. If you got caught, you became a fox and had to help catch other geese. Foxes and geese all had to keep to the paths. The fewer geese and the more foxes there were, the more you had to keep on your toes to stay free. The only place you were safe was at home.

Sarah was awfully good at turning on her toes and twisting away suddenly. She was the very last goose caught! She fell down at last with about five foxes piling on top of her. First they were worried. But when she came up laughing, they helped her beat the snow off her shawl and coat. (It wasn't torn anywhere!) Through the babble she heard Chuckie Gerrick exclaim, "Not even crying! Boy, if that had been Susan!"

And Robbie answered, sort of carelessly, "Oh, Sarah's all right. Pretty tough for a girl."

It made her feel ridiculously happy.

Then the school bell rang and everyone raced across the yard. But Susan was waiting for Sarah at the trampled hub of the wheel.

"You think you're smart, don't you!" she said.

Sarah came to a dead stop. She stared at Susan's face in surprise. Susan had been one of the first geese caught, of course, and she wasn't much of a success as a fox either. She was so chubby. But that was no reason to get mad at Sarah.

"What have I done *now?*" Sarah said hotly. "No, better not tell me. Better go and tell your mama—and let her make a trip to our house and tell my mother, so Mother can tell me."

And Sarah broke into a run again.

Susan was late for class, and her face was absolutely blotchy from crying. But by then Sarah was only a tiny bit sorry for her. Because, the most tremendously exciting thing had happened. Teacher had read Sarah's play, and she said it was by far the best of the lot. She said it couldn't qualify for the prize and that was a pity because Mr. Scott (she meant Keith) had assured her that most of the writing actually was Sarah's work. He had helped with the plotting and the characterization. (What was *that?*) And Teacher said she had asked Mr. Scott to be stage director. She made quite a speech about it—her cheeks almost as pink with excitement as Sarah's.

When Grace and Violetta heard that Keith had promised to help, *they* got all starry-eyed and excited too.

After that Keith came to school for two of the after-three periods a week, and he was very businesslike. Robbie got to be the Irish cook. He didn't care about it, but he was the biggest boy in Braeburn now, so he pretty well *had* to be it. Grace Millar was his wife!

"She's not right for it," said Keith to Sarah on the way home after the first rehearsal. "Not right at all. The only thing in her favor is that she's rather hefty. She's too bold, and she tries too hard to be funny. The Molly O'Grady *I* knew was funny without knowing it. She'd be serious as could be, but the things she said were funny because her husband could twist them any way he pleased. Know anyone at Braeburn who could do the job that way? If she had a trace of an Irish brogue, so much the better."

Susan Gerrick, thought Sarah. Susan was chubby, so that fitted. And both her grandmothers were Irish. She didn't have any imagination—well, not a lot anyway—but she could do Irish readings pretty well. She memorized easily. And she was never silly. She'd try real hard.

But—Sarah wasn't about to suggest that Susan should get the best part in the play!

Susan kept playing Little Annie Sewing, in the basement at recess time with all the little ones, and Sarah joined in the snowball fights on the yard. They had built two dandy forts, and most of the pupils were divided into two armies. This was no game for sissies. The snow was getting heavy with water, so the balls really stung when they splatted on your face.

Spring was coming! March winds blew, and they were special because Sarah's birthday came along to put a final finish to this boisterous, windy, slushy month! It was an exciting thought—she'd be 11 in about four weeks now!

Her play was being prepared for the 17th, and her birthday was coming fast. No wonder March seemed like her month. Her freckles always popped out then, after hiding away during the winter months. And the songs Teacher taught seemed especially meant for her too, somehow. This last one, for example:

"The spring has come; I hear the birds that sing from bush to bush. . . ."

It was a round, with unexpected dips and slurs here and there. Actually, no birds were in sight. Not even one lonesome scrawny crow. But if you had an imagination you could pretend they were, like the song said: "The linnet and the little wren, the blackbird and the thrush. . . ."

Sarah didn't know what a linnet was, but the name sounded interesting, sort of watery and slick. Not like the roads were now. Well, they were watery, all right, but there was nothing slick about them. They were a dreadful mess.

There was as much water as snow now. Wally broke through the crust again and again, but he'd plod on through the slush, then scramble patiently up the next ridge. The sleigh sort of went swimming and tilting along behind. Sarah clung to the dashboard until her knuckles turned white, but she and Robbie were laughing too. You had to keep spitting horse hair. Wally was shedding his winter coat, and the March breezes acted as a curry comb. Loose hair settled on the buffalo robe and brushed past your cheek and floated into your mouth if it happened to be open.

On Sunday a lot of Braeburn people stayed at home because of the roads. The Scotts drove in the big lumber wagon, jolting and tilting along.

Somehow Sarah looked forward to the weekends more than she used to. Not to *Sundays* so much. It was a bit awkward to sit beside Susan in Sunday School, maybe even to share a hymnbook, and not to look at each other or talk to each other. In fact, the Sunday after fox-and-geese day Susan came *on purpose* to sit with Sarah in the evening service. Just as if they were friends! Well, she didn't deserve to be. Sarah simply pretended she wasn't there!

For a moment—just a moment—Sarah caught a peculiar look from Stuart who was in charge that evening. At home that week she half waited for him to mention it, to ask questions maybe. He didn't.

On Saturday Sarah had an exciting surprise. She got to ride to the river with Father and the boys to watch them snaking felled trees out of the woods. With the weather turning so mild and all, this job had to be finished in a hurry. It's always easier to go into the woods on sleds than on wheels. Besides, logs slip more easily on snow than on brush and grass. And this Saturday when Stuart asked Mother to let Sarah come, she agreed right away.

It was Sarah's first time. She had never seen the river hills all patchy with snow like this—close up, that is— with sleigh tracks looping through the woods. She had never watched the way Father and the boys fastened log chains to trees, hitched the horses to the chains, and pulled the logs out of the bush one by one. She had never watched Stuart build a teepee of birch bark on the crumpled old sheet of tin, to start a bonfire at noon. She helped him pile loose branches on the crackling teepee then, and after a while the coals were ready to nest the saucepanful of pork and beans there, with the blackened water kettle next to it. Boy, no *wonder* the kettle got so sooty black. She'd had to scrub it a few times, and that was no simple job.

But this was fun! Her mitts and stockings were soaking wet. (Mother would likely worry about that a bit, she thought.) Father, Keith, and Robbie were busy loading long logs onto the two bobsleds. (She'd get to ride right on top of a load today!) But she and Stuart sat near the fire, talking. She didn't have too many chances because Stuart studied so hard at home.

Somehow Sarah didn't even mind too much when Stuart began asking questions about Susan. (So he *had* noticed!) He wanted to know what was wrong. Why weren't they friends anymore the way they used to be?

Sarah hesitated to tell. Sometimes you have good reasons—*perfectly* good reasons—but, somehow, when you say them aloud they sound sort of—well—*shameful*.

Today when she finally got through speaking she half expected Stuart to say, "Look here. That's no way for Christians to behave."

He didn't. He didn't scold at all. He said, sounding sad and serious and loving. "Is it worth it, Sarah Naomi?"

"What?"

"Holding grudges."

"I'm not!" began Sarah. Then she stopped. "Did Mother talk to you about me?" she said a bit grumpily.

She thought of the evening in the attic. Mother must have talked, and that was why she didn't say Sarah couldn't come out today! Because Stuart was going to—to *preach*. It was like a plot, sort of.

"Does it matter?" he said. "Sarah, we're concerned about you. How can you ask God to forgive you—and all of us need to do that, you know, every day of our lives—how can you do it if you are unwilling to forgive a fellow Christian? Life without the smile of God is a very lonesome life. I *know*, Sarah."

Fortunately, thought Sarah, taking a deep breath, *fortunately* Father and Keith and Robbie were unhitching the teams. It was dinnertime. Stuart quickly measured heaping spoonfuls of coffee into the boiling water, and set the kettle aside. Then he began frying bacon. The bacon and beans were good, and Keith teased her a lot while they were eating, making her laugh. After that she pocketed her apple and went to climb a bald hill.

From there she could look over miles of river with its wide flat fields of ice and snow, and the wooded islands, all black now. The sun and the breeze and the sharp smell of wet poplar were as sad as could be suddenly.

Apples taste about 50 times as good, if you eat them outdoors on a crisp day, as any you eat in school. There you have the smell of chalk and the coal gas and sweeping compound and moccasins with sweaty socks inside and overalls that haven't been washed lately. All of them sort of come crowding in. Today Sarah lingered over every bite, taking deep breaths of clean cold air.

But she couldn't help thinking of her talk with Stuart.

Stuart was sort of special. Ever since last summer when he got right up in church to testify when nobody his age was a Christian. That was the day she got saved—the time Father showed her how, out in the woodshed.

Sarah thought of that day. She was so happy, so happy! It was as if a warm glowing lamp had been lighted inside her so that she'd never, never need to feel alone or afraid any more.

Was that what Stuart meant by "the smile of God on your life"? Without it, he said, life would be lonesome.

This was the frightening thing: *The light had gone out.* Sarah didn't remember just when it had happened, but every day there was this feeling instead—restless and heavy and sad. And *impatient*. She didn't *want* Mother to talk to her about Susan. She didn't *want* Stuart and Mother to talk about her behind her back and to make plans so Stuart could have a talk with Sarah alone.

Take this morning. It was at breakfast that Stuart asked Mother if it wasn't time Sarah got to see how the logging was done. And Mother never mentioned polishing lamps and other Saturday chores. She just said yes, easy as easy.

Suddenly it made Sarah mad just to think of it. Why didn't people just let her *alone?* She didn't *want* to tell Susan she was sorry. She wasn't sorry. It served Susan right. Most of it was her fault anyway—hers and her ma's. At least, well, it was every bit as much their fault as hers.

But what if — What if she kept bearing a grudge the way Aunt Jane Bolton had done for years and years. She never came to church. She had no friends because she was so full of bitterness she couldn't be friendly to anyone.

"Yoo-hoo! Sarah!" The far-off call startled her. She swung to look toward the clearing. Hey! They were ready to leave! In fact, one load, with two figures perched on top, had begun moving along the winding trail. Whee! She'd have to scoot.

Father and Robbie were waiting when she came panting down to join them. With Father's help she climbed the load. He had spread half of a buffalo robe for her to sit on, and he tucked the other half around her knees. Just as the sun dipped to the horizon they began snaking up the mile of river hills. All of them were quiet, so there wasn't much to hear but the swish of the runners cutting through the wet granular snow, and the clink of trace chains. Every once in a while Prince and Captain would snort and toss their heads, but that was all.

At home the usual chores waited. Not the lamps. Mother had finished them. But Brindle had to be milked, and the shoes had to be polished, and Sarah's hair had to be washed, and the dishes had to be dried. Sarah begged to go up to bed before singing time. Because she was sleepy from all the fresh air, she said.

Mother felt her forehead. "Not getting sick again, are you?"

"Of course not," said Sarah.

Mother looked at her soberly. "John, let's have devotions first tonight, before the singing. Then Sarah can have her bath and go to bed."

Sarah was sorry she had mentioned it. Her plan hadn't worked. She'd meant to skip devotions, and it hadn't worked. What was more, she couldn't do any reading tonight. If you were too sleepy to stay up, you were too sleepy to read—that's what Father always said. And Mr. Slocum, their neighbor, had brought their mail from

Blakely tonight. *The Grain Grower's Guide* had come. The doodad page in that was Sarah's favorite. Sleepy Sam, and Flannelfeet the Cop, and the cute twins, Roly and Poly, and the funny crooked chimneys with black cats popping out—it was too bad. They'd have to wait now till *Monday*, most likely.

She chose the footstool to sit on while Father read the chapter tonight. It stood in the corner near the heater, cozy and shadowed.

Lately, no matter what Father read, it always seemed to be a *scolding* piece. Tonight he began, "'O LORD, thou hast searched me, and known me. Thou knowest my downsitting and mine uprising, thou understandest my thought afar off. Thou compassest my path and my lying down, and art acquainted with all my ways'" (Ps. 139).

It was no *use*. Sitting in a dark corner was no use. God saw all, and He knew all. This was *dreadful*.

Maybe, just maybe, King David felt like this one day. He sounded as if he knew all about it. As if he'd been trying to run from God— As if he'd thought of flying to the loneliest island of the sea, *if* he had the wings— And it was no use. God was everywhere!

Father read right down to the last verses: "'Search me, O God, and know my heart: try me, and know my thoughts: and see if there be any wicked way in me, and lead me in the way everlasting.'"

And then everybody prayed. Sarah came last, and she felt as if all her words were dry and crumbly and useless, like sawdust. But she had to pray or the family would wonder why! And maybe they'd guess the real reason.

Maybe they guessed it anyway. Mother held her close tonight for a little minute. But all she said was, "Good night. Have a good sleep."

CHAPTER 8

Spring–and
a Saturday Ride

MUCH OF THE TIME, now that spring was coming,
Sarah found it easy to forget her private troubles. Almost
every day there were new things to see and admire. Calves
and pigs, bawling and squealing, had to be made comfortable. Daisy and Beauty were in foal too, but their
colts wouldn't be born until May. Sarah could hardly
wait. The yearlings were sort of scruffy-looking, not
nearly as cute as baby colts.

This was the time of year when Mother asked Father
to bring the incubator into the house. Most of the year it
was stored on top of the rafters in the granary, so it came
in covered with dust and cobwebs and mouse droppings
and dead flies.

The first thing Mother did was to heat a large panful
of water, and give the incubator a thorough scrubbing
inside and out. The next thing was to fill the lamp and
trim the wick. Then Father carried the incubator down
into the dark cellar.

The cellar was the best place for hatching eggs. The
temperature was pretty much the same day and night,
and the earthen floor didn't tremble when you walked
across it. (Unborn chicks must be terribly particular!)
But to make sure all was well, Mother always had the
lamp going for a few days before she put in the eggs.

The tray could hold 132 eggs. This year Mother wanted to try White Rocks. Mrs. Heathe had some hatching eggs for sale, so Sarah and Robbie were to get them after school this second Friday in March. For the next 21 days the Scott house would have a coal-oil smell. It always did during egg-hatching time.

Sarah was glad Mother planned to put a few settings of eggs under real live hens too. It was fun watching mother hens taking care of their chicks, the round fluffy bits sort of skipping around them. In fact, six hens were sitting already—on goose eggs. That was a mean trick, in a way.

The hens had to sit for four weeks, which was all wrong according to the chicken calendar. The hens must get really worried! But the worst came when their big babies tumbled out of the big shells, and almost as soon as they were dry they headed for the nearest puddle. The mother hens almost went crazy with worry. They just *knew* their awkward babies were going to drown in the water. But they didn't!

Father, who was cleaning wheat this morning, called out to Robbie and Sarah as they drove off to school, "Be sure not to forget the eggs, and be careful not to crack the shells! Don't want to be eating scrambled eggs for a week to come!"

Spring. It was so many things. Icy ridgy roads. A sleigh bumping along, half of the time on frozen ruts of mud, half on tinkling sheets of ice—until Wally broke through the crust. Then you had to watch out not to get speckled with mud all over.

Spring was willow buds beginning to swell in the roadside ditches that were still filled to the brim with ice and dirty snow. It was a bedraggled robin sitting alone on a fence post, looking sort of astonished and forlorn. It was chilly winds, and the lonesome caw of a crow.

At school the snow forts and slides had disappeared. Because of all the mud on the yard, Teacher allowed them to play ball on Grant Millar's hayfield at noon. That wasn't far from school. Most of them trooped over together as soon as the last lunch pail was emptied.

Sarah decided she'd rather read today. Teacher hadn't said you had to go, though even Susan ran out to watch the first softball game of the spring. Sarah was reading *Coral Island*, and she'd come to the most exciting part— where a ship comes sailing—and the three marooned boys, Ralph and Jack and Peterkin, were trying to attract its attention—and they *succeeded*. *Then* they saw the black flag running up the mast, and they knew it was the *Jolly Roger*, a pirate flag! If only they hadn't drawn the attention of the pirates!

They had this secret cave they could go to—but they had to swim partway—and Peterkin couldn't swim!

The schoolroom was very quiet. All the windows and doors were wide open. Teacher aired it every chance she got because this was rubbers-and-wet-socks season, and a crowded schoolroom could get powerfully close-smelling then!

Through the window drifted sounds of yelling and cheering. But indoors there was no sound except the tick-tock of the clock and the rustle of pages as Sarah read on and on.

Suddenly she jumped. Teacher was talking in the hall. Sarah hadn't noticed any footsteps on the porch. And who could be there with Teacher? She was talking quite loudly, as if someone might be standing outdoors under the window. She said something about the coming St.

Patrick's Day program. Braeburn was going to charge admission this time, and the money would go to the Red Cross. It sounded very grown-up and important. Was the thought of the program bothering Teacher?

"I've tried it," Mrs. Millar was saying. "I've tried everything in my power. Whenever possible I have tried to assign them to a job together, so as to break through this silly quarrel, whatever it is."

Right then was when Sarah began to have this funny feeling that Teacher might be talking about her—and Susan.

It was true. Whenever Teacher appointed teams for different cleanup jobs or study jobs—cleaning the blackboards or dusting the ledges, tacking up posters and maps —anything at all—she always had Susan and Sarah working together. It was pretty awkward at times.

"Have you been able to discover the cause?" Grant Millar was speaking! That nice nature-study man. Oh, dear. Now he had to go and know!

Sarah heard Teacher sigh. "I haven't wanted to pry. Whatever it is, these little Christians seem to be pretty thorough in their hating. Remember the old saying, *Behold how they hate one another?* Would you have supposed that cherishing grudges was a Christian virtue?" She laughed as she spoke, but Sarah didn't feel like laughing.

Teacher rang the bell. She came walking into the schoolroom then, and Sarah ducked into the cloakroom through the rear door. Just in time. The other pupils came swarming into the halls, panting and red-cheeked. Oh, dear! Teacher would notice that she hadn't been outdoors. In the confusion she ducked outdoors, scooped up a handful of snow, and rubbed her cheeks and hands with it. Then she raced in, wiping her reddened fingers on her hanky, and took her place along with the noisy ball players.

It was hard to settle down to studying history—all about the battle of Bannockburn. Sarah kept hearing the words *"these little Christians."* Spoken the way Mrs. Millar said them, the words were nothing to be proud of. A lot of Braeburn pupils almost never went to church. Their parents weren't Christians. Everybody knew that she and Susan were supposed to belong to Jesus.

"Behold how they hate one another!"

That wasn't the way the saying was supposed to go. Not long ago Brother Hammond talked about it on Sunday. There was this Roman writer, and he described the early Christians. "Behold how they *love* one another!" he said.

Oh, dear! This was all a *mistake.* She didn't *hate* Susan. It was just *not liking.* There was a difference. But—perhaps others couldn't tell the difference.

Sarah was relieved when school was over. The road was less bumpy this morning because there was less ice and the mud wasn't frozen. But the sled runners had a hard time sliding over the spots where all the snow and ice were gone. The Heathe driveway was the blackest muddy mess of all.

Mrs. Heathe had the eggs packed in a large four-gallon pail. Sarah thought of the road—and of eating scrambled eggs for days. She took the pail on her lap so the bumps and jolts would be cushioned a bit.

Mrs. Heathe was friendly and gossipy as always. She liked to chat with anybody at all, any old time. So she stood in the mud beside the sleigh, her fluffy white hair waving in the breeze. She had one of Mr. Heathe's jackets over her dress and apron, and her hands were tucked into the sleeves. They were probably warmer than Sarah's, in their damp mitts.

"Saw your brother out riding with Louise Thatcher a time or two. Looks like sweethearting, that does."

Sarah felt her heart tightening in that funny way—just as it had when she heard about Herbie liking Kathleen. She was mad as could be that time! Now she *liked* him. And Stuart and Louise—well, they were in grade 12 together in Blakely High School and everything. They'd always been good friends. Last spring when Stuart had to miss school because of the seeding, she rode over every other day or so to bring him his assignments, with a lot of notes prepared so he could study out in the field. Things like that. She was pretty too, with her auburn hair and her fair complexion. Peaches and cream—that's what Mother called it. And she had this erect way of walking, sort of springy. Besides, Stuart was only 18. He wouldn't up and get married for a great while yet.

"Course she's a bit young yet," Mrs. Heathe's tongue was running on. "But some girls grow up faster than others. And with Keith being—how old is he? Twenty-three, is it? I hear tell he's bought Herbie Gerrick's place. Watch those eggs, Sarah."

The pail had almost slipped! Sarah put both arms around it, and she hugged it close. But she felt so bad suddenly, she could have cried into the pail.

When they drove on, she waited for Robbie to say something. Like, "How does silly gossip like that get started?" Or, "Wish they'd keep their tongues at home." She wished he'd say something to show he didn't believe what Mrs. Heathe hinted at. But he didn't. Today he wasn't even whistling through his teeth.

Father came to take the eggs from her, they were so special. And it was a good thing he did. If she'd had to carry them today, even Ginger could have pushed her over. There would have been scrambled eggs on the Scott menu for *weeks*.

Ginger and Spencer always expected a romp, and they came running. It helped Sarah to push troublesome things out of her mind. But when milking time came, and when Keith came to join her, Sarah felt shy of him for some reason.

He was whistling again, a rollicking bit of song. At first Sarah tried to think of the words. Then, suddenly she could—and she wished she couldn't.

> Oh, where have you been, Billy Boy, Billy Boy? . . .
> Oh, I've been to see my wife, she's the joy of my life.
> She's a young thing that cannot leave her mother!

And that silly verse about her age:

> How old may she be, Billy Boy, Billy Boy? . . .
> She is six times seven, twenty-eight and eleven.
> She's a young thing that cannot leave her mother!

Hoo-whee! Eighty-one!

Keith's gay whistling was about all you could hear except the milk frothing into the pails and Ginger's purring and Hyacinth's stamping and Stuart's curry comb where he was brushing Hyacinth and the swishing sound that followed Father wherever he carried forkfuls of hay. All were quiet sounds, sort of. All except the whistling. And in a way that sounded saddest of all.

At the supper table she tried to see Stuart's face without staring straight at him. He was quiet. Not pale though. He'd had to face the wind all the way home from Blakely. It was pretty chilly even if spring was almost here. And his being quiet—well, he usually was. He studied so hard. Mother sometimes complained that he was always so *preoccupied*.

She'd had a letter from Aunt Jane today. There was a long string of things she'd like Father to do before she returned to her farm. Advertise for a good married hired man—that was number one. Air the whole house for a few days, with the fires going. Help the drayman unload some furniture she had ordered. It seemed a pity now that she had sold all her things last fall. And Sarah couldn't help remembering something Mrs. Heathe said:

"Seems almost as if she still thinks of John Scott as the Bolton hired man." Mrs. Heathe sniffed when she said it. Braeburn didn't have a very good memory of Aunt Jane Bolton. All those years and years she'd been pretty snooty to everybody. At least, that's what everybody thought. They didn't know how lonely and unhappy she had been the whole time.

"Isn't it somewhat risky, her coming back?" said Keith, helping himself to a heap of potatoes and pouring gravy over them. "With a broken hip bone, and at her age and all."

"The bone has mended nicely, by all reports."

"Still and all—I don't get the point."

Mother had a strange smile on her face. "I'll read you that part of her letter," she said. And this was the way it went:

I need not remind you, Sheila, what an impression I've left on the community where I've spent most of my life. I cannot undo the past. But by God's grace I'd like to redeem what time is left to me. I'd like to go back to the church where I made my confession of faith years ago, and I'd like to renew the covenant there. I'd like to witness to my neighbors—witness to the change God has worked in my cold and stony heart.

Mother's eyes were shiny when she refolded the letter.

"But doesn't she say anything about Linda?" said Sarah almost pleadingly.

"A few words. Linda is still making what she calls 'satisfactory progress.' That's all."

That could be an indirect way of saying *But don't expect too much.*

That evening Sarah knelt at her window looking over the dark, muddy yard. Spencer was exchanging barks with Slocum's Buster and Heathe's Hobo.

"Be quiet, Spencer!" Sarah commanded softly.

He went *gruff-gruff* a time or two, then quieted down. Sarah laid her forehead on the windowsill close to the three little air holes in the window frame. She felt about the saddest she had ever felt in all her life. She worried about Linda. She thought of how dreadfully long it was since she had had a letter or heard any real news of her. And they were best friends! And she thought with a jumble of feelings about Louise and Stuart and Keith. She loved all three, and she didn't know what to wish for. It would be terrible if Mrs. Heathe was right and if Stuart found out. It would be just as terrible if Keith found out about Stuart—and decided he had better leave home again.

But in a way she was almost glad she had these worries too. They helped her to crowd those other thoughts and words out of her mind.

"Behold how they hate one another."

At the supper table Robbie told a story he read in a newspaper in school. Mrs. Millar always brought their papers along when they got through with them. Grade eight was supposed to read them and find interesting and important news items.

Well, this one was interesting—and horrible. It was about a rich lady in New York who had a panther for a pet, a beautiful black panther from India. She got it when it was a tiny cub, and she raised it, and they were great friends and lived together in her rich apartment. But one day she was found dead and horribly mauled. The apartment was wrecked, and the panther had to be shot.

Sarah thought of the limerick Robbie had recited about the lady of Niger and her tiger. She found herself saying,

> There lived, in the Tropic of Cancer,
> A lady who rode on a panther.

That didn't really rhyme, unless you said it with a lisp.

> There lived in the Tropic of Canther,
> A lady who rode on a panther.

Sarah giggled sadly as she said it that way, because it really wasn't funny.

> They returned from the ride,
> With the lady inthide
> And a thmile on the fathe of the panther.

Her panther was jealousy. And tonight she felt it was about ready to gobble her up. And God seemed so far away. It was frightening. She felt so *alone*.

Next day was Saturday. This time Sarah was sure she'd have a Saturday sort of day, all day. But Father came in at 10 to tell Mother that the yearling colts were missing. And Stuart had suggested that Sarah might help him catch them because the scalawags—that's what Father called them—seemed to answer her call more readily than anyone else's.

"Me? Go riding?" squealed Sarah.

"You—and Stuart. You'll have Wally, of course."

Oh, *Wally*. He wasn't built for comfortable riding. But Keith had ridden Masquerade to his new farm. He planned to make a survey to see how much of the land he'd need to farm, because he had to get the seed ready. A lot of that land was native grass. It and the winding creek made the place just right for raising horses, he thought. But he said he'd have to see it.

Stuart and Sarah had quite a time finding out which way the yearlings had gone. Most of the snow that was left around the house and barn was trampled badly. They rode in a sort of half-mile circle—not a real circle, because fences barred their way here and there. It was Sarah who picked up the trail. She was proud and pleased about that.

The yearlings had been in Slocum's yard and had pulled some bundles out of the stack of feed. That was a naughty thing. Then they'd been over at Heathes' and then they wandered north again, and west. Stuart and Sarah followed the trail. It was pretty clear now.

This road going west wasn't used very often, especially in winter. Sarah remembered that during part of last summer she had taken this road to school so she wouldn't have to pass Aunt Jane's place. She was so mad at Linda!

Instead of turning south toward Braeburn school though, the trail led west. And now they were on the way

to the place where she and Keith had been riding that exciting Saturday when the bull chased Louise.

She was thinking of Keith and Louise—and suddenly— there they were! Riding along together! She couldn't *believe* it.

The yearlings were there too. Keith must have lassoed them. So they were safely caught.

Stuart had reined in Hyacinth. "Guess we're not needed," he said. "Come, Princess."

He turned and rode away quickly, behind the nearest screen of bushes. Wally went lumbering after. All Sarah could see of Stuart was his back. He kept going and kept going, never turning. His voice, when he spoke that one time, sounded awfully husky. Sarah followed him sorrowfully.

After about a half mile, Stuart half turned.

"See how blue the river hills are today?" When she

didn't answer, he looked around. His voice changed. "Well, Sarah! Hey, no need to look like this, sis. The end of the world hasn't come."

She couldn't help asking, "Is it—is it *very* bad, Stuart?"

The muscles in his cheeks jumped. "Sometimes." She could just barely hear the one word.

So then they sat there, just sat for a minute, looking at the blue hills.

"I don't want to grow up!" Sarah burst out suddenly. "I don't want to be older than 10, not ever. It's too sad."

Stuart gave a little laugh. "Not much you and I can do about that, Sarah Naomi. Time passes, and we age along with it. But here's something to remember: 'Jesus Christ the same yesterday, and today and forever' (Heb. 13:8). He never changes. Look, Sarah—whatever you know or think you know, don't speak to Keith about it. Promise?"

She nodded. And she thought, *"Behold how they love one another."*

"Let's go home," said Stuart.

"No, wait."

It wasn't easy, and it wasn't *going* to be easy. But she had to do it, and suddenly she *wanted* to do it. "I've got to see Susan. Come with me, Stuart. OK?"

A bright smile washed over his face. "OK! As you say!"

CHAPTER 9
Sarah and Susan

IT WAS ALMOST 12 o'clock, so Sarah and Stuart rode home pretty fast. Not really fast enough though. Sarah felt as if she could fly, she was so happy.

"Let's sing," she called. "Hey, what'll we sing?"

"Anything except that 'Billy Boy' thing!" said Stuart. Then he stared into her puckered face, and the next minute they were laughing together. And that minute Sarah felt better about Stuart—heaps better.

"*You* seem chipper enough," he remarked. "How about telling me what happened back there?"

Well, part of it he knew, of course. He was there with her when they met Mrs. Gerrick sort of striding across the yard. She always had this—this *purposeful walk*. That's what Father called it. It always looked especially purposeful when she was tending the stock at home— feeding chickens and slopping pigs—that sort of thing. She wore a large denim jacket, and a denim cap with a visor pulled low over her forehead, and sort of mannish leather gloves."

"Well, Stuart!" Real friendly. "And Sarah." She gave Sarah a sharpish look.

This took all the courage Sarah had. "Could I—may I see Susan?"

"I suppose so. Yes. yes. I'll go with—"

106

But Stuart pretended not to hear the last part. " I hear your prize brood sow has produced a record litter," he said.

She smiled proudly. "Seventeen healthy young. Care to see them?"

"Very much."

So Sarah got to walk to the house alone.

"And do you know what?" she said to Stuart now.

"No. What?"

"Susan simply couldn't believe me when I said I'd been jealous of her. She said *she* was jealous of *me*."

"Imagine that!" said Stuart, but he smiled a peculiar smile.

"And know something else? When you're sorry about what you've said and done, and the other person is sorry about what she's said and done, why, there's nothing to untangle. Just nothing!"

"And so it's all cleared away, is it?"

"All—except— Do you suppose I should have said something to Susan's ma too?"

It was a bothersome question. She had never said wrong things or acted in wrong ways to Mrs. Gerrick. But she had been mad at her because she thought her a meddler.

"How do you feel toward her at this moment?" said Stuart.

Sarah thought about it. The sore feeling was gone—all gone. Sarah remembered the kind look Susan's ma gave her when the two girls came out of the house hand in hand. Maybe some people don't need words. Mrs. Gerrick had been upset over Susan. Now Susan would tell her mother the whole thing, so that was all right.

"I'll race you home!" said Sarah suddenly.

Of course, Wally couldn't keep up with Hyacinth, but he tried. She and Stuart were laughing breathlessly as they rode up to the barn at home and dismounted.

A Saturday sort of dinner waited for them. A lot of odds and ends of leftovers all tossed into a pot and turned into a mulligan stew. But there were creamed peas besides, and hot biscuits, with canned peaches for dessert.

Stuart must have explained about where they had seen the colts—to Father out in the barn. At the table no one talked about them. Keith brought them home in the afternoon. He'd had dinner at Thatchers, he told mother, looking happy. And when he came to help at milking time, he was whistling "Billy Boy" again!

Sarah poked her head around Brindle's hock. "Hey, how about whistling something else?" she said. "For a change."

He looked startled and amused. "Have I been boring Your Highness? Sorry. What is your command?"

"Do that Irish medley we're singing on the program."

But that reminded Keith of the play—their play—and the way Grace Millar was spoiling it. Teacher herself had groaned several times and wished there was *someone* who could take Grace's place.

Sarah's heart skipped a beat. "Is it too late to change? Because, if not, you could maybe try Susan—Susan Gerrick."

"The *no-imagination* girl?" He didn't believe she was serious.

"Well, she memorizes real easy," said Sarah eagerly. "She wouldn't go stumbling and giggling along the way Grace always does. She'd know it, every word. And she's chubby, so that fits. And she doesn't know when she's funny, and—"

"Well! Sounds promising! But why haven't you mentioned this possibility before? If you hadn't been my sister and Robbie's sister too— But it would hardly do for a Scott to direct the play and two Scotts to take leading parts—especially as it was you who wrote the thing—"

"And you," said Sarah.

"Anyway, thanks for the tip, sis. We'll give it a try."

Sarah could hardly wait till Monday.

With the road so bad and all, riding was the best way to travel now, so all three rode to school together. They arrived a bit early, on purpose. First Keith had a private talk with Teacher. As soon as school began she asked Grace and Susan to go to the hall. Mr. Scott wished to speak to them there.

Sarah grinned to see Susan's face—it was sort of *stunned*.

She wished she could be there to hear what Keith said. He was going to give a solo part to Grace because she had a nice voice, but Susan would be Molly O'Grady. He had her read parts, and she even put in the right Irish expression, all serious and nervous as she was. When she came back to the classroom, looking more stunned than ever, she was excused from all class recitations for the rest of the week so that she could memorize her part. She and Robbie went over their scenes during schooltime too, and Sarah got to be prompter.

She was glad for her friend, but one thing bothered her. She couldn't forget Teacher and the *Behold-how-these-Christians-hate-one-another* thing.

"Well, why don't we go and tell her?" proposed Susan at recesstime.

"Tell her what?"

"*Everything*." Susan had a lot of common sense; that's what Herbie always said. And that's exactly the way she

sounded now. "We'll tell her what we quarreled about, and that it was no way for Christians to do, and that we're sorry, and that we're good friends again. Come on!"

Being bossy isn't so bad if it's done in the right way and at the right time and for the right reason.

Teacher looked up from her work at the two girls who stood side by side before her.

"Well?" she said. "Anything wrong now?" She had an *on-guard* look, sort of waiting for trouble, or something.

Sarah wished Susan would speak up now, but she only squeezed Sarah's hand.

"Well," began Sarah stumblingly, "I—I heard what you said to Mr. Millar on Friday. That about Christians hating each other—"

Mrs. Millar got red. "Eavesdropping?" she said, making little pencil marks on the sheet before her. *Eaves-*

dropping was something she was pretty strict about. She didn't approve of it at all.

"I didn't mean to," said Sarah. "I didn't *try* to."

"Did you try not to?" said Teacher. "And I still can't see—"

"Why, Teacher, can't you see?" burst out Susan. "We're *friends* again." She pulled Sarah's arm up so Teacher could see they were holding hands. "We were sorry, and we apologized, and now we're friends. As good as new."

"I—see."

"And I'm not sorry I heard what you said." Sarah looked earnestly at Teacher. "Because Christians ought to love each other. And—and now we do."

"I see. Well, that's nice, I'm sure," said Teacher weakly. But Sarah saw her eyes looked sort of misty.

"I guess that's all," said Susan. taking a deep breath. "Let's go play, Sarah."

"Where?" It was just a question. Nobody had to avoid anybody now. Nobody *had* to play in the basement because she didn't want to run into a certain somebody outside! Certain somebodies were friends again. It was a rich feeling.

But Susan said, "Do you *mind* playing with the grade-one children?"

"Do you *like* playing Little Annie Sewing all the time?" Sarah asked, astonished.

Teacher was laughing now. "But I thought you just got through saying you were friends again!"

"We are," said Susan, "but we've got to talk this over. Come."

On the way to the basement she said she had *promised* to play with them. See? She had to keep her promise. See? So she'd tell them that tomorrow they'd play alone.

That way they'd *know* and they wouldn't be *disappointed,* see?

Ah, it wasn't so bad. The little ones were surprised and pleased to have Sarah Naomi play with them, so she had to be Little Annie Sewing in her little housie this time. She squatted in the middle of the ring, and she pretended to cry when they went around and around singing, "Nobody comes to see her except her little mousie." And they giggled so, they could hardly sing the rest:

> Rise, Annie, rise! and
> Shut up your eyes; and
> Point to the east, and
> Point to the west, and
> Point to the very one that you love best!

Susan's voice was higher from the floor than anyone else's. Sarah pointed right smack at the place where it came from. It was just a game, but Susan was pleased.

That week was a dreadfully busy one. Every afternoon —all afternoon—Braeburn school rehearsed for the program. Any pupil who wasn't rehearsing at any time was busy cutting out decorations—hundreds of green shamrocks, brown potatoes, and black top hats; dozens of fat pink pigs, chubby ladies in red cloaks, and men in baggy trousers and wooden clogs. Some of the shamrocks were for people to wear after they paid admission. The rest of the cutouts were glued to windows and walls, to the bookcase and map case, anywhere and everywhere. The place looked real fancy, especially after the stencils were done.

There's a special feeling about stencils on the school blackboards—a holiday sort of feeling. They proclaim, *No classwork. No homework. This is fun time.*

First you wash all the boards so they look black as black. Next you tack the stencils in place—the pictures with all the lines pricked out with pinpricks. Then you pat the dusty brushes gently over all the lines. And when the stencil comes off—there's the picture. There were peat bogs and cottages, and Irish colleens and gossoons—that's Irish for girls and boys—but the Irish sounds a lot gayer.

The most special part of all this year was that Susan and Sarah got to do two of the stencils by themselves. Susan was so neat and careful; she was an awfully good partner. And when they had followed all the lines with colored chalk, the pictures looked lovely.

Monday evening brought more excitement for Sarah. Mr. and Mrs. Grant Millar came riding into the Scott yard for a call. Teacher wanted Father to sing two solos at the program. She had them all chosen for him too: "I'll Take You Home Again, Kathleen," and "When Irish Eyes Are Smiling."

Sarah grinned; she was so proud of Father. He could sing those songs the way they should be sung. She knew he could. But Father didn't promise. He wanted time to think it over, he said. And when Grant Millar and Teacher had gone again, he said he didn't know if he should take part in this foolishness.

"A frolic is not necessarily foolish," said Mother, rocking gently as she knitted new heels to a pair of Father's socks. "There's no law that says a Sunday School superintendent must not laugh or cause others to laugh, is there?"

Father smiled, but then he turned sober again. "To turn the life of one of God's choice missionaries into a figure of fun and nonsense— I don't know if I should have a part in that."

"Missionary!" said Sarah, astonished.

"There! What did I tell you?" exclaimed Father. "Doesn't know a thing about St. Patrick, I warrant."

"Tell Father what you know about him," urged Mother, smiling a funny little smile.

"Well," said Sarah, "there's Ireland in there somewhere —and snakes—and a staff, I *think*—and—and—"

"See?" said Father.

So then he told the story, the way it really happened about 16 hundred years ago.

This was a chilly evening, so the heater in the parlor was burning. The door leading to the kitchen was open, and there Stuart and Robbie and Keith were reading or studying. But here there was no lamp—only flickering firelight and shadows. Mother's rockers squeaked, and her needles clicked, glittering in the firelight. Father's voice sort of wafted Sarah away. *Wafted* was a lovely magic-carpet sort of word that fitted exactly.

There was this happy little Scottish boy—*Scottish*. He wasn't Irish at all! One day he was kidnapped and taken across the sea to Ireland, where he was sold as a slave to an Irish chief. He had to take care of a flock of sheep. He didn't like being a slave, not one bit. So he ran away —and was recaptured. But the next time he ran away, he was too smart and quick for them and got away, clear to France. He went to school there, and finally he came back home.

Then—when he was free and grown-up—he said God was calling him to return to Ireland to be a missionary to his former enemies. Ireland had hardly any Christians at all then; the people were followers of the Druids. Patrick's parents and friends begged him not to go, but he went! He went around preaching outdoors, and the rich and poor flocked to hear him. There was a great revival, bigger than the one Braeburn had last year! *Hundreds* of churches were started. Patrick also began schools where men could study about preaching and teaching the people.

So that was who St. Patrick was. He preached in Ireland for about 35 years! So what did that have to do with pink pigs and brown potatoes and green shamrocks? Father wanted to know. What did that have to do with top hats and peat bogs?

"This," said Mother gently. "Patrick became more Irish than the Irish in order to save Irishmen. And that's scriptural, you'll have to admit, John. It's in the great tradition of the apostle Paul. 'For unto the Greeks I became a Greek.' And what is more Irish than pork and praties?"

"Your mother is a clever woman, Princess," said Father, pinching Sarah's cheek. "Too clever for this simple farmer."

So Sarah guessed that the matter was pretty well settled. Father would take part in the frolic, and the very next day in Sunday School he probably would tell the story of St. Patrick to all the boys and girls. Sarah thought they would probably listen all the better because they had heard him singing about Irish eyes.

People came to the program in spite of the muddy roads. They came from *miles* away, a lot of them on horseback or in wagons. Robbie sold tickets at the door, and Grace and Violetta pinned on the shamrocks.

Then when the last seat on the last bench was taken, and the sidewalls and the back were lined two-deep with people *standing*, the three ducked down into the basement where Teacher and the other Braeburn pupils were waiting. Upstairs there were a couple of hissing Coleman lamps, glaring as could be. Down here there was nothing but a smoky lantern. Everybody was jittery, with Teacher giving last-minute instructions. They were all just about *sure* they would forget all they were supposed to remember.

Then, 7 o'clock! Two by two, Braeburn school marched up the creaking steps and onto the clanking plank platform. The program had begun.

First came the songs and recitations and dialogues. Sarah had parts in two dialogues. Not her own. That came last of all, and everything was planned to *build toward* it— that's what Teacher had said this morning. Well, Sarah's nervousness was building toward it too.

Father's solos were lovely. Everybody thought so. They clapped like anything.

And then came the final play: "Molly O'Grady's Mulligan Stew" by Sarah and Keith Scott.

Sarah sat with the other pupils near the front, and her fingernails bit into her palms, she was so nervous. Then Robbie and Susan—Tim and Molly O'Grady—came on stage for their first scene. It was funny. Susan said her lines, serious as could be. But it was funny. The people laughed at almost everything she said. She didn't know why, and she looked astonished—and that made everything funnier and funnier.

Suddenly Sarah felt someone grab her hand. She glanced over her shoulder, and there was Susan's ma, looking pleased and shiny-eyed. The squeeze said, *"Thank you for being friends with Susan again."* And it said, *"My, isn't she doing a good job!"*

And she was. So Sarah squeezed back just as hard. It was nice to be friends again with Susan's ma too.

After the program, the mothers of Braeburn served a lunch. It was a dreadful crush—hot and noisy and close-packed. Now that the excitement was over, Sarah had a pounding headache, and her insides seemed to be on a boat, rocking and tilting. She didn't dare touch any food. Not a thing. All those lovely, lovely cakes and tarts!

She was relieved when Father came wading through the crowd to say that it was time the Scott family left for home so they would be on time for Sunday School next morning.

Just that minute someone tapped Sarah's shoulder. There stood Teacher with Keith and Louise Thatcher and a strange man. He was big and chubby and sort of bald —that was all she could really notice.

"So *you're* the author," said the man. He was Mr. McDonnell, the former Braeburn farmer who thought up the whole contest idea! "Too bad you can't have the prize. You surely deserve it. But since the rules forbid, I'd like to give you this recognition." And he pinned a blue ribbon to her dress!

The circle of smiles became sort of blurry, and the roomful of people began spinning faster and faster. Father's voice came through a peculiar roaring, and it was strong and comforting.

"I think," it said, "I think I'd better take this lady home. She's had quite a day."

The cold air helped. She felt a lot better outdoors. But Father wouldn't let her ride Wally home. She had to get on Prince, in front of him.

"Who has a better right than the Prairie Princess?" said Father.

Prince wasn't a very good riding horse, but Mother had Hyacinth. The road was rutty with frozen mud and ice, but a pale moon shone, so that was all right.

Sarah was glad the day was over.

CHAPTER 10
The
Thirty-first of March

FOR A WHILE, school seemed dreadfully flat and every-dayish after the St. Patrick's Day program. Mrs. Millar had to be stricter than usual because nobody felt like working. The weather was foggy and chilly day after day too. The whole world had this dark, dirty look, it seemed to Sarah. Nothing was *happening*. The sun wasn't shining. The remainder of the snow wasn't melting. Spring was at a standstill.

Home was sort of flat too. But Sarah secretly knew why it seemed so. Her birthday was awfully close, but nobody seemed to be *remembering*.

Now March 31 is a silly sort of day for a birthday, any way you look at it. An April Fool kind of day. The roads were always messy then, so there was never any idea of having a birthday party. Once—just *once*—Sarah would like to have a party, with cake and ice cream and games. But she had stopped wishing for one long ago.

She always received a present, a little something. Father couldn't afford big presents. Maybe a new dress. Her winter serge had had to be patched at the elbows *twice*. In other years Kathleen had always baked a cake for her, but Kathleen wasn't here now. Would anybody else remember?

Another worry was that she hadn't heard from Linda

Bolton in weeks and weeks. She had sort of hoped Linda might remember March 31. That was part of her worry. But mostly it had to do with Linda herself. Was she worse? Wasn't she going to walk after all? Why didn't Aunt Jane write about her or *for* her if Linda was too ill to write her own letters? Aunt Jane wrote plenty of letters. All of them had to do with things Father should do to get the farm ready for her coming.

He had advertised in the *Paxton Observer* for a married hired man. And he went to Paxton a number of times just to see some of the men who answered the advertisement. There were four or five, but all of them so far were men who had almost no farming experience, or who had farmed only in England. Methods and seasons are so different, and Aunt Jane wouldn't be strong enough and active enough to train them herself. And Father said he wouldn't have time to train a green hired man for her. She'd have to have a dependable man.

The day before her birthday, Sarah and Robbie rode home through unusually thick fog. Days were pretty long now. Fog makes a difference though; it crowds in. You go tunneling through, sort of, and the tunnel opens foot by foot in front of you, and closes in right behind you again. And if you're feeling happy, that's all right. The fog shuts the happiness in with you, all nice and cozy and private. But if gloom is riding with you, boy, that fog is *really* gloomy!

So Sarah came into the house rather quietly. She stood just inside the kitchen door and sniffed. Coal oil, from the incubator in the cellar. *No vanilla and chocolate smells.* No Kathleen—no cake. She sighed. Well, there was still tomorrow.

"Sarah?" called Mother from the bedroom. "Is that you?

Run down cellar for some vegetables as soon as you've changed."

The changing didn't make much sense. Twice-patched serge isn't exactly precious, it seemed to her. But if you were a Scott you *changed* after school, and that was that. Of course, she'd rather be a Scott than a Siddons. They *never* changed. And look at how shiny their sleeves were with dirt! Not Violetta; she was neat. Susan's ma said it was a marvel how that girl kept herself so clean in that pigsty of a home!

Going down cellar was sort of interesting nowadays because of the incubator. You didn't need a lantern now. A dim light always came through the long panel of glass in front. You could see the tray with its rows and rows of eggs. Mother lifted it out every day to cool the eggs for a bit, and to turn the eggs over and sprinkle on some water. That seemed a funny thing to do. But Mother said Sarah should watch a real live mother hen. She always left the nest for a while to feed and drink. With damp feet and feathers she'd go scratching around in the nest then to move the eggs around a bit before she sat down on them again. To get a good hatch you've got to imitate the mother hen.

Sarah knelt on the earthen floor for a while, peering in at the eggs, thinking. By Sunday or Monday they should be breaking out of their shells! So maybe she could have a chick for her birthday present.

Mother called again, reminding Sarah to hurry, so she scrambled to her feet. The light seemed to be growing stronger, but that was because her eyes had grown used to the cellar now. She could see the vegetables in their bins. Potatoes, carrots, a turnip, onions—that sounded like stew. And stew wasn't Sarah's favorite food.

"Better get the milking done," said Mother briskly when Sarah set the basketful of vegetables on the kitchen table. "Keith asked me to tell you to bring all four pails when you come."

Sarah ventured, half hoping, "Did Father go to Blakely?"

"He's been there—and back. Sorry, no mail for you. Now run along."

The cows were grouped around the trough outdoors. In the barn Keith was carrying great forkloads of straw and spreading it all over the area where the cows usually stood or lay down. This was to keep them warm and dry and *clean* so that the milk would be clean too. The gutters were all cleaned out, and the aisles swept, neat as anything. But Keith wasn't whistling at his job today. Maybe he felt the fog too.

Sarah went to rescue Speckle's egg just before the cows came swaying into the barn. Each knew her own place and swung into it, waiting patiently then to be fastened into her stanchion. Sarah stood ready with the three-legged stool clutched in one hand, and the pail dangling from the other, as Brindle took her place. Someone else stood waiting too— *two* someones. Speckles and Ginger. The hen flew to the top of the stanchion, hopped onto Brindle's head, and walked deliberately along her backbone and settled down on her big footwarmer. But Ginger sat behind Brindle, and began staring expectantly at Sarah.

The first twin streams of milk came purring into Sarah's pail. Pretty soon the bottom was covered, and foam began forming. When there's foam, that shows you're getting to be a pretty good milker. Fast!

Ginger begged for a share, as usual. Suddenly Speckles

hopped onto Sarah's shoulder, and peered down.

"Wha-a-a-a-a-a-t in the w-a-a-a-a-a-r-ld a-a-a-re you do-ing tha-a-a-a-r?" she asked in her complaining voice.

"Feeding Ginger, of course," said Sarah.

"What's that?" said Keith, sounding startled.

Sarah laughed. "I was answering Speckles. She's a nosy gossip. And she doesn't know that *world* isn't spelled with an *a!* She says wa-a-a-a-rld."

"Probably she's Irish," said Keith, joining in the fun for the moment. But then he lapsed into silence again. Come to think of it, he wasn't nearly as cheerful nowadays as he used to be. Why, she hadn't heard him whistling for days and days!

When Sarah finished milking, she got up.

"Wait a minute, Princess, if you don't mind," said Keith. "I'd like to talk to you. Here, I'll hang that pailful of milk up so it'll be out of harm's way."

They hung side by side—his pailful and hers. But Keith fiddled thoughtfully with the hayfork for a while. He looked troubled, she thought.

"Grace Millar said something to me the other night," he said then.

Grace Millar!

"She said—she asked me how it felt to—to steal my own brother's girl away. She must mean Louise. Louise is—well, she's a girl in a million. I've thought so ever since that day— Well, *you* know, Princess. You were there. And you're a knowing youngster for your age. Tell me, do you know anything about it? Have I messed up things for Stuart?"

That was a difficult question—a *terribly* difficult question. She wished he hadn't asked it. But after a moment Sarah remembered something Stuart said to her. *Nobody can spoil your life except you.* And she shared that with Keith.

"So you see, you didn't. You can't have."

"When did he say this? Where?"

"Oh, we were out riding. L-looking for the y-yearlings—"

"Aha!" said Keith. "Now we're getting somewhere. Did you and Stuart see Louse and me that morning?"

She nodded unhappily. "But—but we went away quickly. And—and then we talked. And because of what Stuart said, suddenly I knew I had to go and see Susan, and he came with me. Now we're friends again, Susan and I."

"That's Stuart for you. That's the way he affects you." Keith's voice was husky. "Quiet strength, that's what he has. Tell me some of the things he told you—if they're not too private."

So she told him. About being afraid to grow up. About that verse, "Jesus Christ the same yesterday, and today, and forever."

Just then they saw Stuart dismounting from Hyacinth's back near the barn. He was back from high school, so there was no more chance for Sarah and Keith to talk. But Sarah wondered if maybe her brothers had a long private talk. Mother kept supper waiting, and nobody made any comment about that. Of course, stew can't really spoil, so it was a good thing Mother had planned that for tonight. But Sarah had this funny feeling—as if a storm cloud was hanging over the house, with everybody waiting and waiting for the first thunderclap. Then Stuart and Keith came in, and they were talking naturally, even laughing a bit. Sarah took a deep breath. The storm cloud, if it had been there at all, had broken up and drifted away. It seemed as if everybody was breathing easier.

But—no one mentioned a birthday coming up!

Stew for supper—then dishes to wash. And Mother mixing yeast for overnight buns. (That meant more bowls and spoons to wash!) And Father mending harnesses, getting ready for spring. Mother didn't really like him to do it in the kitchen, but he sort of liked to have company when he was doing this job, and the smithy was an awfully chilly and damp place now. Stuart helped Keith with some problems, and Robbie read his supplementary readings. It must be nice to be in grade eight! You had to read ever so many storybooks, so nobody told you to put them aside and get at your homework. This *was* Robbie's homework!

By and by, bedtime came. Sarah said good-night and ran upstairs in the dark. She thought, *I'll never be 10 years old again. This time tomorrow, I'll be 11 years and one day old!* It was a funny feeling, tingly and sort of sad like.

When she had slipped into her flannel gown she went to kneel beside the window. She opened the little sash with its three round air holes and placed her lips close to one.

"Spencer?" she called softly.

"Whuff!" He'd heard!

"Good night, Spencer!"

"Whuff!"

She thought of last birthday. She was dreadfully little then! So many things had happened since. Linda's coming —and Kathleen's getting engaged. She'd been a silly to be so mad at Herbie for wanting Kathleen! And there was the revival, and that really was the most important happening of all. She thought of Aunt Jane's accident and Linda's coming here to stay.

And she thought of threshing time, and of the day when Linda got saved! And then Kathleen's wedding and her going away with Herbie. And Father and Mother leaving for Ontario before the big October blizzard struck. And the coming of "Jack English" who turned out to be her very own brother Keith. So many good things, all crowded into one year!

"Thank You, God," she whispered. "I guess I don't really need any present. Why, You've been sending them all year. A best friend—and a brother-in-law—and a brother—and Susan and me being good friends again now, better than ever. Thank You. And I guess I'm not afraid of being 11. Because You'll be there too."

Jesus Christ, the same yesterday, and today, and for ever.

So Sarah Naomi Scott went to bed, and she slept through to her birthday.

No one wished her a happy one—no one sang to her that morning. There was the usual before-school busyness so that she and Robbie wouldn't be late. She heard Father and Mother talk about a trip to Paxton. So probably they wouldn't even go to Blakely—just *in case* there might be a letter or parcel from Kathleen and Herbie, or from Linda.

In school Susan was friendly, and they talked about many things. They talked about April Fool jokes, since April Fool's always came the day after Sarah's birthday. But Susan didn't mention a thing.

Sarah and Robbie reached home before Mother and Father did. Keith was tending the stove when she stepped into the kitchen. Sarah sniffed. Roast goose. *That* seemed just a bit special. Keith seemed to be in a dreadful hurry to go milking though. It was earlier than usual. And out in the barn today he was whistling "Billy Boy" again. He must really be happy; he whistled so loudly. Must be nice to be happy. Probably Stuart told him to go ahead and have Louise for his girl if he wanted to—and if she wanted him!

"What's *that*?" said Sarah, cocking her ears suddenly.

"Well," said Robbie, who was carrying feed to all the horse mangers, "if you don't know that song *yet*, after all the times Keith has whistled it!"

Keith laughed and told Robbie to be more respectful of his elders.

"Hush! I don't mean the whistle!" said Sarah. "Listen! It sounds like a *car*."

"Well, why not? said Robbie. "I saw Mr. Heathe out in his yesterday."

"Driving through all the mud?" She couldn't believe it.

"Well, mostly the mud is frozen solid. The road must be dreadfully bumpy though."

Sarah was getting up to run for a peek, but Keith told her she'd better tend to business. (He was getting terribly bossy!) They didn't want to delay supper on her account, he said.

"Why, Mother and Father aren't even *home* yet," she said, astonished. But she settled down to finish Brindle. Then she and Keith carried the milk to the kitchen. It was getting dark, so Sarah started for the parlor to get a lamp.

"Better get out of those milking clothes and start peeling potatoes," said Keith. "A lamp? I'll go for one."

Mother and Father came home soon after. Father was very chatty tonight, telling Keith in detail about the man he interviewed today. He sounded promising. Father thought Aunt Jane would have just the right man there.

"A Ukrainian, but he's worked on a Canadian farm for a few years. Seems willing and dependable."

Robbie came in, then Stuart. They were all here together in the kitchen. And nobody—no single body—had remembered what day this was!

Then the door to the parlor opened slowly. Sarah turned and stood staring. Her hands flew to her mouth, and she couldn't say a single word.

Linda. There she stood, smiling. Faces crowded the doorway behind her, but they didn't matter just then. Nobody mattered but Linda.

She came walking on her own feet.

"*Linda, Linda, oh, Linda!*" Sarah was laughing and crying as she flew to meet her friend.

"Careful," warned Father. "Don't throw her off her feet!"

As if she would have! But, oh, it was good to put her arms around her best friend.

"Now walk again," she said eagerly. "Let me see you do it!"

Oh, she had prayed and prayed for it to happen, and now it was happening. Linda swayed a bit. She'd always have a slight limp, but she could walk.

That minute someone began singing—*all* were singing: "Happy birthday to you!" Linda, the tall man with the receding forehead (the way the books describe it) and Aunt Jane—Susan, her ma and pa— Why, this was a birthday party!

Sarah was so giddy, she twirled around and around on her toes.

"Oops, there," said Father. "Remember, you're 11 now!" But he was laughing as hard as the others.

"I thought nobody remembered—except God."

"Well, we did our best to keep it secret. We went to Paxton to meet Linda and her dad and Aunt Jane—and the Gerricks offered to bring them out in their car."

So that was what Sarah heard! "But where's the car now?"

"Behind the strawstack," said Keith. He'd been afraid she'd notice the tracks on the yard though, so he came to the house with her to occupy her thoughts—and to keep her out of the parlor.

"Know something?" she told him with a grin. "I thought you were dreadfully bossy."

Well, then the party began. Mrs. Gerrick helped Mother add more boards to the table and spread the good damask cloth. Imagine! Sarah and Susan counted noses—three Boltons, three Gerricks, and six Scotts. Twelve. That's a real party. They put on the overnight buns. (Now Sarah knew why Mother baked that kind. So she'd be free to go to Paxton today.) Father carved the goose, and everybody helped put on the vegetables and pickles and things. Even Linda carried the filled water glasses, to show she could do it.

Her dad was nice, not stiff or anything. And Aunt Jane talked as freely as anyone. It was like a dream. Sarah could hardly eat; she was so excited. Then Mr. Gerrick rose and brought in an ice-cream freezer just chock full of squishy homemade vanilla ice cream. While Mother was dishing it up, Mrs. Gerrick brought in a four-layer cake with 12 candles on it. One to grow on, she said, because Sarah had begun her twelfth year today.

The surprises weren't over. There was a letter from Kathleen and a small parcel that came all the way from California—*real* artificial silk stockings, the kind Susan wore for best. There were new sandals from Mother and Father and a lovely piece of brocaded crepe. Blue. Sarah fingered it lovingly. It would make a beautiful Sunday dress for summer. And Susan gave her a box of hankies and a little bottle of cologne.

Robbie and Stuart had gone out. Robbie called Sarah to the door now. There in the lantern light she saw a pony. Black, graceful, slender-legged, but sturdy looking too.

"A present from Linda and Jane," said Mr. Bolton pleasantly. "A little token of thanks and appreciation."

"Well, it's really from Dad, mostly," said Linda.

"For *me?*"

Sarah couldn't believe it. She felt almost like a sleepwalker when she moved down the porch steps and the pony took a step closer and sniffed her hands. She stepped really close then and ran her hand over the pony's neck and along her jawline.

"What'll you name her?" called Father from the doorway.

The name came in a flash. "Panther," said Sarah breathlessly. "Black Panther."

They thought it a funny name. Mr. Bolton tried not to smile, but he reminded her that she needn't choose in a hurry. This pony was a gentle lady. There was nothing bloodthirsty about her!

"You wouldn't *mind*, would you, sir? I could call her Blackie."

"No, of course not. If that's your pleasure."

She thought maybe Robbie understood, in a way. He gave her a peculiar look. The pony would always remind her of some things she needed to remember.

"Hey, don't go in yet," said Robbie. He slipped a tooled

leather saddle on Black Panther's back. This was a gift from Keith and Stuart and himself, he said.

All of them—*all of them*—planning to make her birthday perfect! And it was.

"Ready for more ice cream, anybody?" called Mr. Gerrick. "Let's eat it before it melts, folks."

And they did.